I0831706

Scramble

Education is a matter of life or death.

Fred Williams

WILLIAMS INDEPENDENT PUBLISHING

ISBN: 978-0-578-70213-1

Email me @ fw1685@gmail.com

Acknowledgments

To all the hardworking men who inspired me to work hard, and to all the women who worked miracles.

To my family and friends who had the tough conversations.

To my first editor Joyce Joiner.

To Babe...H.O.M.H.F

Chapter (9x9)-(9x8)-((3x2)+2)

Dr. Clark H. Watson, Ph.D. Mathematics

Tchaikovsky's "1812 Overture," Opus 49, opened a beautiful sunrise in the east as I pulled into the gas station for my daily cup of coffee and bagel. I tried every gas station in St. Louis and this was the only place that makes my coffee the way I want it. Before the start of school, I delighted myself with hazelnut cream with a dark roasted bean. *Today, I want something that will energize me,* I thought. I heard the crunch of pebbles between the ridges of my Stacy Adams shoes as I opened the door and greeted the station attendant.

"Good morning to you. It looks to be another splendid day."

"Well, good morning to you, too, sir," she said.

Scramble

"Punctuality is the habit that breeds success. The early bird gets the worm." I laughed while she leaned against the counter with a curious expression on her face.

"Do I know you from somewhere?"

"You ask me that every time I come in here," I said.

"I know, I know, but your face rings a bell."

While walking to the breakfast aisle next to the cashier, I lowered the brim of my hat to rest on my glasses. The aroma of fresh hazelnut dissolved as the smell of bleach and cleanser she used to clean the station prior to my arrival rose from the floor. She must have just finished mopping. I pressed the dispenser handle and watched the paper cup fill to the edge, moments from spilling.

I took a sip and burned myself.

"Ouch. Underestimated the temperature. I forgot to convert to Fahrenheit before I started drinking. Don't you hate it when that happens?" I said, attempting more banter.

Today, she smiled. Maybe she felt sorry for me. I liked her curly red hair and how it bounced off her shoulders—longer than it had been in the days she'd lined up third from the back to go outside. I sealed the rim of the cup with the plastic lid, reached for a piece of wax paper, and instinctively took an oatmeal-raisin bagel. Reconsidering, I set it back in the row of pastries and grabbed a poppy seed bagel. No, that's not it either.

Scramble

I examined the Long John, glazed doughnut, jelly-filled doughnut, coffee cake, and a Boston crème pie that was hard as a hockey puck. After a few minutes evaluating the case, I determined I didn't want any of them. Dammit, too many to choose from. Perhaps a sandwich? *Sounds delicious, but I don't have enough money.* Oatmeal-raisin won the contest as I hurried over to the register so the attendant could ring my items, remembering to grab a newspaper from the stand to my right.

"Sir, are you okay? Got a little frustrated there picking a doughnut, I see."

She laughed, but I didn't see anything funny.

"Allergies bothering you today? Your eyes are bloodshot."

She tried again to rattle me, but I remained focused, waiting for my total.

"Alrighty then, let's see... the usual. I should have this memorized by now." The attendant smiled again, almost embarrassed.

"Take your time." I sipped my caffeinated delight, now the perfect temperature, while she tapped on the computer's touch screen to total my items for this day, and the other forty-three consecutive days I had begun my mornings there.

"Bagel, coffee, and newspaper is..."

Scramble

"Three dollars and twenty-three cents," I finished her sentence. "Just like yesterday." I smiled again and gave her a five-dollar bill. I predicted today would be a productive one.

"Oh, by the way, I'll need that back in all nickels, please. The staff at school came up with a clever idea of having the kids collect nickels for St. Louis Children's Hospital for cancer research."

She stood there bewildered by the request. Her blank expression resembled a computer when the screen freezes. She had the same look of confusion she did when she sat in room C-11, row two, seat seven from the left. Her hair had grown well past her shoulders. I waited patiently while she stared at the touch screen, then at me, then the screen again, hoping I would change my mind. *No! Today I change* your *mind.*

I repeated, "All nickels would be great."

"Give me just a second here... let me think," she said.

"Is something wrong?" I asked, tapping my hand on the counter, waiting for my thirty-five nickels and two pennies.

"Give me a second so I can get this right." She reached for a calculator, and I sternly interrupted her move with my voice.

"Excuse me. You can't tell me the amount of change?"

"Yes, it's $1.77. I'm just having a rough time with the ol' brain. It's early."

I stepped closer, concluding she got that number from the big bold letters on the computer screen. She had given me a one-dollar bill, three quarters, and two pennies for the past forty-three days. It's a shame she hadn't listened to me seventeen years ago when I calculated the amount of my bagel and coffee in a question I asked her in math class. She didn't have an answer then, just like she doesn't now. I warned her it would cost her later if she didn't understand math. Just like yesterday's news, they forget as soon as the bell rings. My patience had grown restless.

"Anna, I must leave. I showed you this."

"We barely have enough nickels."

"I don't think you know." Distance equals one meter.

"I'm sorry. Give me a minute here."

"Anna, they're just nickels. Count by fives."

She counted them out while I used the minute she requested to survey the store for cameras. Two. One above the register and the second in the northeast corner. I checked outside for early birds pumping gas. As usual, no one was disciplined enough to get up at 4:45 a.m. Their inability to set their alarms would cost Anna her life in nickels. I calculated the angle of penetration between the 2.5 inches of her unzipped jacket. Fifteen degrees with a slight tilt accounting for her two feet of elevation at the counter. I had given her enough time for redemption and she chose not to utilize the opportunity.

Scramble

"Anna Madsen, class of 1993, first grade at Happy Canyon Elementary School, you can't tell me how many nickels are in $1.77?"

"Wait a minute, how'd you know my name?"

I pulled out my gun and she shrieked, dropping whatever change she had accumulated to the floor. The sound of the crashing coins irritated my ears as I counted fifteen five-cent pieces dancing across the linoleum. I waited for the rolling coins to be silent, then continued.

"I ask the questions here; you fucking understand me?"

"Sir, sir... please don't kill me. What do you want?"

She put her hands up as if I wanted to rob her. What an insult. This wasn't a robbery, this was a test, and I wanted my answer.

"Didn't I say I ask the questions? Now answer me. You've got one try to get it right. Think. How many nickels are there in $1.77?"

She started crying. I stepped closer. Distance equals a half meter.

"I—I—I don't know."

"Pathetic."

I shot her in the abdomen and kept firing while I began an oration on money matters. The nuances of my lecture became muffled as the bullet tore through her shirt like a hot comb on tangled hair. Her eyes rolled back when bullet three hit her, causing her to keel over from the force of the shots. I reached across the counter for her right jacket sleeve, steadying her with my left hand, and pulled her into the fire until my gun emptied. I punched my arm forward in anger with each shot that pierced her stomach. Thank god for suppressors.

"I told you seventeen years ago there were twenty nickels in a dollar. How dare you insult me? Your math is important. Didn't I tell you that? Answer me, goddammit."

By this time, I had let go and she slumped forward over the counter. Such a waste of a brain. I couldn't bear that her life ended in confusion so I lifted her head up by her hair and whispered, "The correct change is thirty-five nickels and two pennies. Good day!"

I dropped her head and grabbed my cup, wiping the blood-saturated base. I stepped back and admired my masterpiece. *I am ridding the world of stupidity one clip at a time.* I checked my watch. No time to clean up unless I was willing to risk running late for school. I wasn't. I reached for my cellphone and pushed two, which speed-dialed the tailor.

"Hello."

"Good morning. How are you this fine day?" I asked.

"Watson? Do you know what time it is?"

"I made a mess and I wish to place an order."

"This early in the morning?"

"Yes, I have a few stains on my new shirt. I am aware of the inconvenience but the sooner you can stitch me up a replacement, the better," I said.

"Watson, I require a 24-hour notice. Hold on, let me get a pen. What is your neck size?" I heard him cough a few times in the background. Time has caught up to us both. Unbidden, the thought came that I'd known him for a long time, and I still don't know his name.

"Oh, I'd guess five feet, three inches. Somewhere between one hundred and thirty, and one hundred and forty pounds," I replied, giving Anna an impassive once-over.

"Sleeve?"

"Citi-Gas on Kingshighway and Holly Hills."

Out of the corner of my eye, I noticed the headlights of a car pulling in. The brewer signaled that fresh coffee was ready. I refilled, expecting the customer to walk in so I could inform the tailor I needed two shirts.

"Chest size?"

"None so far. A green minivan just pulled up right now."

"Shit."

The customer driving the minivan slid his card into the credit machine and pulled back.

"Cancel the chest size, he's paying at the pump."

"Okay, okay, good. Cut the lights after they leave. Lock the front entrance and hang the closed sign on the door. Unlock the back door."

"Will do."

"Next, what is your shirt length?"

"I am running late for work," I replied.

"Lack of planning on your part does not constitute an emergency on mine. You're probably rubbing your birthmark. I swear you will rub the skin off that thing. Shirt length, please."

I took a deep breath, absorbing the truth in his words. My finger had traced the scratch on my head a few times already. I saw him in my mind, swinging his glasses around by the arm of his frames while the other hand ran through his receding hairline. The tailor's calm, gritty voice raised my blood pressure as I scanned the scene I created.

"The floor, counter, cash register, and a few drops splattered on snack items sitting next to the register," I responded as the driver in the van pulled away. I walked to the door to get a look at my former student's vehicle. The bell clanged like lunchtime as I flipped the "open for business" sign and let it slam back against the glass door.

"Wrist?"

I looked up again to confirm the store's cameras.

"Two, one in the northeast corner and one above the register."

"Bicep?"

"Toyota Prius, license plate number, 7UFL453."

"Type of fit?"

"As soon as possible. Damn it, I grabbed her head in anger."

"Okay, the butcher will be extra as you know. He hasn't had breakfast in a long time. I'll be there to pick up in ten to fifteen minutes. Throw the circuit breaker and cut power to the building. I will call you with the total so you can wire me the funds."

"Thanks for helping me on short notice."

He exhaled over the phone.

"Next time give me a day's notice. Preferably two." He paused a moment, then continued, "We need to chat when you are free. Something important has come up."

"We don't chat. We have nothing to chat about. Stitch my shirts, please." I cut him off and hung up.

I whistled "Capriccio Italien Op. 45," another masterpiece by Tchaikovsky on my way back to the car, saddened by Anna's refusal to learn. Her disinterest had spoiled my appetite—not to mention that she fell on my bagel. I went home and changed clothes, ready for a fresh start.

Later that morning.

"Wit liporetee and jusdis for awl."

I saw the glossy eyes, blank mouths—bet none of them understood or even had a remote idea what they chanted. As soon as I made it home to change into a clean suit, Toni Holtgrew, the kindergarten teacher, called to say she was running late. Rather than coach her on punctuality, I used the opportunity to lecture this class of rising stars. By that I mean, teach them something applicable to their adult life. They assembled in a circle on the floor. Miniature backpacks and jackets filled the classroom of Happy Canyon Elementary Kindergarten Room 1. Boxes full of toys lined the walls. Toys? Why buy distractions when priority lies in enhancing focus by reading books. Plastic chairs mimicking boxes of crayons sat under the desks the teachers used for skills work. The alphabet lined the wall above the chalkboard; upper and lower cases of A to Z bound by proper lines of height. Three black chalkboards stationed around the room held bright colors of chalk. I stood at the center blackboard and I drew a clock.

"Good morning, class!"

"Good morning."

"Who are you?" Dion Wheels inquired, pushing her purple glasses back on her cardboard brown face.

"I am your principal, Dr. Watson. Good morning," I said.

"Good morning, Dockter Watson," they recited together.

"Good morning. Your teacher, Mrs. Holtgrew, is running a few minutes late for class and I will be—"

"Good afternoon!"

"Who said that?" I asked smilingly while they giggled.

"I did," Arina Jacobs raised a hand shaking with excitement. Her hair was pulled back into a blowout afro puff secured with pink fabric bands. She wore a shirt proclaiming "I Love Elmo" paired with a denim skirt.

"Stand up," I said. She rocked herself up to her feet. I put both of my hands on my thighs and stooped down.

"Name?"

"My name is Arina Jacobs. I am five years old."

"Very good. Arina, you said good afternoon. Why?"

"It was funny."

"I've got a funny question for you." I leaned forward, ready to challenge her math. "Arina, are you smart?"

She put both her hands on her hips with sass. "Yes, I am. My mom calls me a smart ass every day."

"Oh," I snickered, not expecting that answer.

"She said a dirty word. Oooooooh!" Michelle Fields, wearing a Snow White and the Seven Dwarfs dress, exclaimed. Michelle's hair hung right below her neckline and matched Snow White's dark tone. Other kids chimed in, passing judgment on Arina's replay of what her mom had said. Fault lies with parental guidance. Vina Bates. Happy Canyon 1991, room twelve, row eight, seat two due to disciplinary issue.

"Five seconds... four... three... two ... one." The ruckus that started with Arina's comment died down to silence by the time I reached one.

"Class, remember you only talk when your hand is raised, right?"

"Yes, Dockter Watson," they said in unison like a choir saying "amen."

"Good. Arina. Simple question. What time is it? Point to it on the clock." She took a quick peek at her pink wristwatch and pointed to the number eight. Note: Analog to digital clock conversion skills—above average.

"Eight o'clock." She clapped her hands when I nodded.

"Good." I turned to the chalkboard and drew the hour hand on the eight and the minute hand on the twelve.

"Now, tell me what time afternoon begins?"

Arina put her finger on the dimple of her cheek and swiveled her hips, trying to guess the answer for a moment. She looked up, blushing.

"She don't know the answer," Michelle blurted out.

"Yes, I do! It's twelve o'clock."

Impressive. Note: Exceptional display of critical reasoning skills under pressure with numerical recognition from a phonetic identifier.

"Arina did an outstanding job. Let's give her a round of applause."

The students cheered as Arina blushed from the well-deserved attention. Note: Fields displays jealousy. Low confidence demonstrated by hands crossed. Same as her female parental figure, possibly root cause of self-esteem issues.

I pushed the envelope of my child Einstein.

"Next question, Arina. How much time is between eight o'clock and twelve o'clock?"

She sat there again, scooting her hips back and forth without moving her feet. I used the moment to hush Juan Adams, who was leaning over, talking out of turn to Sean Shrugs. Two swings every two seconds for the mini-human metronome. I pointed to him, and he stopped immediately.

"One! Two! Three! Four! Four!" Arina started jumping up and down like she was the next contestant on *The Price is Right*.

"Four hours? Right! Point to the start of the afternoon on the clock on the board."

Scramble

Arina ran up and pressed my perfect clock with her finger, smudging the chalk. I could see her fingerprint where she pressed. She turned and spoke in her cartoon voice.

"My uncle lives in California. He is in the Spacific Time Zone. Let me see, uh, it's six o'clock out there."

"Arina, you know what a time zone is?"

"There are twenty-four hours in a day. The earth rotates three hundred sixty degrees per day. That means the earth travels fourteen—mean fifteen—degrees per hour. We have six time zones in the United States including Huh-wy-hee, and A-lass-ka."

She smiled. I smiled.

Challenge passed.

Note: Will review notes and submit inquiry for grade promotion. Subject has excellent memory recollection. Parental deaths canceled due to superb home school reinforcement of advanced learning skills.

"Very good job. Now sit down, Arina."

"Dockter Watson, you have something on your shews."

"Hmmm?" I looked down and in memory heard the crack of Anna's skull when I slammed her head down on the counter at the gas station. Arina is such a refreshing one-eighty from this morning.

"Oh, that? Ketchup. I had ketchup with an old friend this morning. Very observant. Now you better scoot before I catch up to you!" Arina scurried to her seat as her giggles filled the room like air freshener. She high-fived Mary Huber sitting next to her. Dammit, Watson, you forgot to wipe your shoes. Arina's comment reminded me to check with the tailor to make sure my new shirt was ready. I continued my lesson in basic chronology.

"Okay, let's learn together what Arina did in her brilliant mind. Let's use our hands. Class, now join me. Put your hands out. No fingers up."

Arina and fourteen other students stuck their tiny fists out in front of their beaming faces. Collin Williams stuck his leg out and raised it.

One by one they raised a single finger while they counted, following my commanding voice.

"Start with the number eight. Ready—go! Eight to nine... nine to ten... ten to eleven... eleven to twelve!

"Now class, here is the tricky part. Who wants to try my trick question?"

A slew of hands flew up so fast, their arms jumped out of their sockets. I almost picked McDavid Kay, but I chose my friend in the Snow White dress.

"Okay, you with the Snow White dress. Stand up."

Snow White stood up and stuck her tongue out at Rosetta Hodges. *Education must triumph over misbehavior!* She gracefully strolled to the front. Distance equals two meters.

"First, we do not stick our tongues out in class."

"I'm sorry, Dockter Watson."

I knelt and whispered in her ear.

"Michelle, the next time you do that you will hold your bloody tongue in your hand, unable to call for help. My knife is in my pocket. Understand?"

"Yes." Michelle looked at me like I was the monster under her bed. She clenched her fist weeping as a thin line began dribbling down her leg.

"Good. I scared you. Now stand in the corner until your sock is dry," I whispered.

I stood back up while she marched into the corner near the coats.

"Okay class, help Snow White out. I need a new volunteer." The group quieted, confused by Michelle's abrupt dismissal. "Oh, I'm sorry. I guess the cat got your tongue. What's your name?" I asked the child in front of me. I noticed the princess theme was popular with my youthful students. They were not princesses. They were intelligent women who would learn to work hard for the better in things in life, starting now.

"My name is Dion. I'm a princess too."

"Yes, you are, Dion. Excuse me, your highness, Princess Dion." Dion had long flowing blonde hair. Her eyes were deep blue. The class giggled as Dion made her way to the front of the class in a lavender dress with glitter. "The subjects in the Royal Court would like to know what time the Princess's lunch feast is?" I asked, adding some British accent into my voice.

"Is it twelve a.m. or twelve p.m.?" I continued.

Dion smiled at me. She caught her glasses sliding down her face and adjusted them with a slight push.

"That's a hard question."

"No, it isn't. Now think." My British accent left the room with my smile. My stare was a dart and her face was the board. Mother: Darcy Wheels, Class of 1989 Happy Canyon Elementary, room seven, row sixteen, seat two. Strengths: Social Studies, Reading, History, and English. Weaknesses: Math and Science. The fruit does not fall far from the tree. I had asked Dion's mother the same question years ago and gotten the same look. I would challenge Darcy's math the next time she picked up her stupid daughter. After two minutes, I was losing the attention of the class to fidgety activity. I put my finger to my lips to tell them to be quiet.

"Princess, the subjects are waiting. A.m. or p.m.?"

"I don't know."

"Answer the question, Dion."

Swiveling must be a thing for kids. I knelt before her swiveling highness, pointing my finger right between her eyes.

Scramble

"Princess Dion, I am issuing a royal decree. You have fifteen years to figure out what the abbreviations a.m. and p.m. stand for. Education is serious for a princess. Don't disappoint me. I'd hate for royalty to go missing. There will be many jealous kings and queens who will want to overthrow a dumb princess. Not under my tutelage. You are just as smart and capable as Prince Charming. You will manage your time and it begins by knowing basic chronological skills. Ask your mommy and daddy. Keep asking until you figure it out. Study. Once you know it, don't forget it, you understand me? I will come riding back into your life on my white horse, in shining armor. I will get the answer to my question. If I don't get my answer, someone is not waking up from her beauty sleep. Got it?"

"Yes sir, Dockter Watson." She looked sad. But she must learn now while she still has a chance.

"Class, time's up! Your teacher is here," I said.

I groaned from the pain that shot out of my kneecaps as I rose to my feet. The teacher, Toni Holtgrew, hung her coat on the hanger while I noted that dealing with five- and six-year-old hyperactive kids takes a toll on the body. The excited schoolchildren crowded around her. I walked to the door to see myself out when she stopped me, stepping over the pile of little monsters.

"Thanks for covering for me," she said.

"My pleasure. We need to talk about Arina. She belongs on a higher academic playing field."

"Yes, she does. Yesterday, she told me the chemical composition of table salt down to the valence electrons of the sodium and chlorine. I am afraid of what else is buzzing in that mind of hers. I've already made an appointment with her parents to discuss. I'll send you the invite." She glanced at my clock on the chalkboard. "Were you trying to teach on a first-grade level again? Kids aren't required to learn time standards until next year."

"Yes, I did. I think they need to prepare for what's ahead in their academic career. Arina's participation today was music to my ears. On another note, I am going to the urban league meeting tonight. Did you want to go?"

She raised an eyebrow.

"Why are you going?"

"They are hosting the National Society of Black Educators this weekend. Dr. Melody Xavier is the guest speaker tonight," I replied.

"And this interests you?" she asked.

"I know I'm a principal, but it's good to keep a fresh perspective on teacher issues to make sure we don't march to the beat of a different drummer. I support a harmonious principal–teacher working relationship."

"I hate to change the tone of this conversation, but I have to decline the offer. I have plans with a few girlfriends tonight."

"Oh, where are you heading to?"

"A new restaurant in the Delmar Loop called Pi."

"As in apple pie?"

"No, it's quite clever. It's called Pi, based on the Greek symbol, but they specialize in pizza. Like pizza pies."

"Well, that is clever. What does Pi represent in math, Toni?"

"Something to do with a circle. I haven't had math in years." She laughed it off, but I didn't see anything funny. While she was failing to define the ratio of the circumference to the diameter, my phone vibrated. It was the tailor telling me my shirt was finished and ready to go. I relaxed a little but angered at my teacher reciting nonsense in my presence.

"Don't you know what Pi stands for?"

"Off the top of my head I couldn't tell you."

"You should know better, Toni." *I should cut off the top of her head*, I thought while rubbing the blade of my knife in my pocket. *I can't believe I have to subject my ears to this nonsense.* I pressed my thumb on the blade until I could feel the pain of my skin ready to break. Toni stood there in awe as my temper boiled at her ignorance.

"I'll ask you again. Toni, what does Pi represent?" Distance equals one meter. Her smile turned upside down into a frown at my refusal to let her out of the conversation.

"Dockter, will you teach time again?" Juni Khudjan surprised me, tugging on my pant leg. She looked up with a smile. I refrained from challenging Toni's understanding of the most beautiful ratio in the world and made a mental note to revisit this later in the year during teacher evaluations.

"Yes, Juni. Soon. Toni, your class is waiting."

"Let me know how the meeting goes," Toni said, smiling again, and turned to begin her class. I leaned against the door to give Princess Dion one last look before leaving. When she turns twenty-one, her knight in shining armor will be there to kill her happily ever after.

Chapter 2

Ava Minnow

"Isaiah! Shut up crying, or I'll give you something to cry about!"

I yanked my belt off like a ripcord to a parachute which made Isaiah, my son, cry harder. He knew a whipping was coming because I used his first name. His nickname is Dazzo, after the word dazzle, given to him after he spoke his first words five months after his birth at St. Matthews-Mercy Hospital in St. Louis. Isaiah is on his way to being someone special. Cursing is a bump in his life that a few bumps on his behind will take care of.

"What did you call your teacher?"

He didn't answer, so I lassoed my Gucci belt and popped his butt like bubble gum.

"Answer me."

"The B-word."

"Who are you calling a bitch?"

He tried to whisper his guilty answer. I ruined that idea. I felt that wrinkle connect my two eyebrows as I swung the belt three times across his arm. He cried so hard he had snot running down his lip. He tried to wipe it off in the middle of one of my swings—a bad idea.

"Put your hands on the desk."

"Mama."

"Don't 'Mama' me. Where did you get that word from?"

He didn't answer, so I popped him on the behind again, again, and again. I knew the answer to that question. *Who is Isaiah Sr., Alex?* I thought, pretending I answered the *Jeopardy!* host in the form of a question. I would bet my empty savings account Isaiah Sr. referred to me by that term. Dazzo probably overheard him during one of our many arguments about rules that need enforcing that ain't when he gets his son for the weekend. Homework don't get done and I know it's because they play those video games. I had to ground Dazzo for a month before because of a streak of poor grades.

"Ms. Minnow, I think that's enough."

Excuse me! Wait a minute, Ava. No, she didn't tell me what to do with my child, did she? I stopped tanning Isaiah's butt for just a moment and felt that wrinkle again. I turned to face his teacher, Miss Colwell, with one hand on my hip. Oh, she acts like she disapproves, but I'm only doing what they are afraid of.

What my parents did to me and what Isaiah Davis Jr. needs today. I looked over her shoulder to the principal, Dr. Watson, who stood behind her in the dull, beige room. In it sat one desk with no papers; only a single office phone. The blinds were pulled halfway to show through to a walkway a few teachers were using on their smoke breaks. We had excused ourselves from the reception area of the principal's office to take care of Dazzo's punishment. I invited them to come in, which they obliged. Based on the looks of their faces, his principal expected this; his teacher did not.

"Excuse me?" I asked incredulously.

"I think he learned his lesson."

"Miss Colwell, I really don't give a damn what you think." I stopped myself from finishing my sentence with "bitch".

"Last time I checked his complexion, you were not his mother. Your opinion has no value to me. You called me up here because he called you a bitch, and I will make sure it never happens again. Everything—the name-calling, a waste of a day's pay, and the quarter tank of gas I used to come get him will be taken out on his behind. Do you understand me? I don't need your two-cent opinion on how I love my child."

"I'm calling the police."

Miss Colwell grabbed the phone and as fast as she grabbed it, it slammed back on the receiver by Dr. Watson, who snatched it from her. He frowned at Miss Colwell, whose head only reached the middle of the sky blue and green checkerboard necktie hanging from the dressed-to-impress principal. I saw a look of disapproval in his eyes beyond his round glasses, which were sitting above a well-trimmed goatee. He shook his head with a resounding no, whispered something in Miss Colwell's ear, and they both walked out. I hoped he whispered, "Mind your own fucking business before she minds it for you." He quickly turned back to me and nodded. My pains subsided.

I see why Dazzo called her a bitch.

Chest pains! *Relax for a second. Get yourself together, girl.* I felt my eyes well up with tears from the strain of trying to regain control of my breathing. *Talk to him for a second while you calm down, Ava.* I put one hand on the desk next to where Dazzo had assumed the position. *I told you, girl, to get checked out while you got medical benefits,* I thought. Okay... okay. Take deep breaths. I could see the cracked door of the nurse's station through the glass pane in the office door and remembered my mom's cure for everything: two Tylenol and a Sprite. Don't have a headache, stomachache, backache, diarrhea, polio, chickenpox, or a broken leg. She would drive up to the school and give you two Tylenol and a Sprite, then send you back to class. I need two and a Sprite for these chest pains. I almost laughed out loud.

"Isaiah Davis, look at me."

Snot ran from his lips as he whimpered. I pointed my belt in his face.

"I hate doing this, Dazzo. I can't afford to come up here because you cuss out the teacher and call her a bad name. We are trying to save for your college education and the new house. Remember the new house I showed you? This is costing me so much. This will cost you more if you don't listen to me. You must respect authority or Mama's whipping ain't gon' be nothing compared to jail, you understand me?"

He didn't respond.

"Do you understand me?" I leaned in closer.

"Yes, ma'am."

"Now turn around so I can finish."

"Mama, please."

"Don't 'Mama' me. Do as you're told, boy."

I started whipping him again, but not with the energy I had before. I wanted to direct that energy now to his teacher, who'd tried to educate me on how to raise my son. *Stick to the students, bitch.* I could see the reflection of the receptionist's desk from the closed door's window in the unoccupied office we were in. Miss Colwell wiped a stream of tears from her face. Why's she crying? I didn't know. She must have felt guilty for what she caused. She should have been happy she would be getting a new Dazzo sitting in her class. Oh well, her tears would not stop a club and a cop having an unpleasant day. I continued for another minute, then called it a day. We both walked out to the receptionist's desk to meet Ms. Colwell holding crumpled tissue. I pushed him forward.

"Apologize, Isaiah."

He sniffed.

"I'm sorry."

"What's your punishment?"

She looked up at me, surprised he had more in store after seeing that display of T.L.C.

"One month no PlayStation, TV, or playing outside."

"Ms. Minnow, he's not that—"

She stopped mid-sentence and looked at Dr. Watson, who shook his head. She turned and grabbed her purse, mumbling something as she walked away, upset. I think I heard "he's not that bad of a kid," or something. She probably only got time-out in her youth. They've got time-out for black men; it's called twenty-to-life. She walked to the door and turned to Dazzo.

"Isaiah, I'll see you Monday and we'll have a fresh start, okay?"

He stood there mad at her, which I don't blame him for, but he had to respect her. I shoved him again.

"You must want another whipping, don'cha, boy?"

"No, ma'am."

"Your teacher said goodbye, now answer her."

"Goodbye."

She wiped her eyes and stormed down the hall. Probably to report me to family services. She doesn't understand he's my baby, and I loved my mama to death for the whippings she gave me. I would be dead or somewhere in an alley strung out on drugs if she hadn't instilled values in me. I was walking out the door when Dr. Watson called out to me.

"Ms. Minnow."

"Dr. Watson." I turned and tugged Dazzo to prevent him from going further.

"You're doing what's not being done enough to these kids. I'm sick of families denying their kids discipline. Life teaches hard lessons and some you can't walk away from so easily. I'll speak with Miss Colwell, and I look forward to us meeting again on a more positive note. It takes a village."

He reached out to shake my hand and I obliged. Damn, my mama always said that. I couldn't stop thinking about Mama as I rushed to the car to get home. At least I could get a head start on dinner. While we were driving, I had to wipe my own eyes twice when I looked back and saw how droopy Dazzo's face looked. *He will achieve more than me and go to school*, I promised myself. *Tuition these days runs north of at least one to two hundred thousand dollars. The price is running up and running with good tennis shoes. I know he'll need scholarships, but I need to make more money at work to help.* I laughed, thinking back to my own childhood as he sat leaned over on one side to avoid the pain from welts. *Maybe I'll give him some butter pecan ice cream after dinner.*

I'd calmed down by the time I looked over at the dashboard of my car. The check engine light flashed on. Damn it, my stress returned like a boomerang. Problems, my biggest crush. It always showed up when I really didn't want to see it, just like my baby's daddy, and they both ask for money. *Money, huh? I guess child support is out of the question.* That has disappeared for the past five years, too, but I got a running tally on him. *Don't drop the soap in jail, you delinquent dad*, I laughed wickedly to myself. The engine idled erratically as I pulled up to our apartment. I put it in park and yanked on the emergency brake next to the console between the seats. Piece of crap has been a bigger headache than Dazzo from the moment I signed the contract. Brakes, tires, oil light, check engine, radiator leak, alternator... you name it, and I got it replaced on this lemon. Isaiah Sr. called it a "failure of research and development." *Someday*, I promised, *I will have a new car to park in front of my dream home.* I looked at Dazzo's long face.

"Get in the house and go to your room. If it needs electricity, then I don't want it on. Understand me?"

"Yes, ma'am."

He got out and slammed the door. *Ava girl, what is the problem? Your chest and car are both acting up.* I caressed my chest until the sharp pains resided. The doctor told me to cut my salt down last year. My blood pressure was high, but nothing of concern just yet. Dr. Kevinsky insisted I change up my diet and get rid of the pork rinds. God on earth, I love pork rinds. I had to smack Dazzo's hand when he tried to reach into my bag.

Man, I hoped it was nothing serious with this car. Now wasn't the time. Time to turn it off and let it rest. Maybe that would calm it down. I got out and walked to the steps of our two-bedroom apartment. I heard local rapper Az-Zhan playing in my next-door neighbor's apartment. That's all he ever played was Az-Zhan. That rapper killed more people on vinyl than heart disease and breast cancer joint. I heard his last album blaring through the walls, as he bragged about the crossing guard he filled with bullets. *What issue do you have with a crossing guard? What? Are kids taking too long walking across the street?* I commented to myself. Too bad he got shot and killed earlier this year behind a nightclub. Life imitates art. I laughed as gunshots rang out behind the baseline on his song.

I banged on the wall and the volume went down. My neighbor, Bachari Haids, had been living next to me for a few years. I know he sells, but he doesn't bring it around the apartment, and I appreciate that. We'd spoken several times in the laundry room and he'd told me he does his dirt, and that ain't shit kids need to see. I don't let Dazzo go anywhere near him. Someone might have an address on him and Dazzo won't be a casualty playing at the wrong place at the wrong time. Bachari didn't plan on being in the game too much longer, he told me a few weeks ago as he dumped Tide into the washer. Much longer is right because I was about ready to call the police on him.

On another washing day, Bachari explained how he got his nickname Spaghetti. His mom had walked in on him shoving spaghetti up his younger sister's nose, and thus he earned his nickname. Plus a free ass whipping. He said it just like that.

I walked into my apartment and saw the flashing light on the answering machine. I told myself to face the music, so I pushed Play.

My voicemail picked up and said, "Please enter your passcode." I punched in Dazzo's birth date. Voicemail woman then said, "You have twenty-two unheard messages... first message..."

"City Sewer calling regarding account number—" I hit the pound key to continue.

"Second message."

"This is City Water calling for—" I hit the pound sign again. I'd send water twenty bucks, so they'd know I was trying.

"Third message."

"Hello, this is City Electric calling about—" I'd sent them thirty bucks. What the hell did they want? I thought I broke my nail when my index finger hit the pound sign.

"Fourth message."

"Hey, Boo. This Isaiah. Call me when you get a second."

What do you want? I said to myself.

A phone call interrupted my voicemail box. I paused, not sure if I wanted to answer. I let the number show up on caller ID. My best friend, C-note. I called her C-note but her government name is Columbia Calle. "Hello," I said it like I was talking to a stranger.

"Sup, bitch?" She always said hi like that. I half-smiled because she's always in a good mood; I'd met her ten years ago at a Mexican grocery store. Columbia Calle is big, jolly, and from the Dominican Republic.

"Sup with you?"

"You alright, *amiga*?"

"Girl, let me tell you 'bout this bitch at Dazzo school. First, I get a call talking about Dazzo actin' a straight fool—" A clicking sound interrupted the call. "Sorry, my phone was acting up—anyway bitch gon' tell me that's enough while I was wuppin' his ass."

"No, she didn't, girl. Did she?"

"Yeah, talking about he ain't that bad of a child. I looked at her ready to wup her ass for showing out in front of the principal, you know?"

"*¡La nervia!*"

"C, I finished wuppin' that little brown ass. She won't have that problem again."

"*¡Mi compañera!*" She started laughing.

"How was your day, girl?" I asked. I looked at the stove, chanting for greens, cornbread, and chicken to magically appear. The longer I looked, the longer I realized I'm not a magician. I pulled some corn out the freezer while C went on about some trainer who kept looking down her shirt. I laughed when she said he'd said, "I'll see you guys later," and she was the only one standing there.

"Ask him out. He must like you."

"I don't know, *vieja*. He's kinda weird. I'll wait a few weeks and see what's up his sleeve."

"Don't wait too long, Chiquita."

I cursed the phone company as my line started clicking again. I said a few more things and ended my call with C so I could start dinner. I looked back at the stove to see if a full-course steak meal had appeared. To hell with hocus-pocus.

Chapter 3

Le'Angelo Brooks
One year ago

When I awoke, I was sitting in a chair with my hands tied behind my back, facing the man no one in St. Louis fucks with, Osbourne. That's all he goes by. No one knows if that is his first or last name. He had the look of death when I stared into the eyes of my captor. He's an older gentleman with square glasses but damn he can wear a suit. Charcoal gray outfit down to the shoes. Even a gray shirt with a gray tie. He's a polished man. He was reading some paperwork when his office phone rang.

"Yes, that is fine. I'll send one of my men to pick it up. Great doing business with you," he said and hung up the phone.

He had about four of these calls in the half-hour I sat there, as the blisters from the ropes scorched on my hands. We were in an office that sat above an abandoned warehouse. The city skyline and the moonlight reflected off the river through the windows. It smelled like mothballs and pesticides. I wasn't sure what was in this place, but I could tell Osbourne's drug traffic filled most of the boxes stacked high in here.

I remember walking out the back door after robbing Becky's Grocery Store. I gave the money back that evening but I had blacked out sometime later. Grandmama. The hospital had called to inform Jonas that Grandmama was unresponsive, and they'd placed her on the breathing machine. I was sure he'd be there by now. I should be too. Memories of my loving Grandmama came to the surface and created more energy as I wrestled the chair and rope securing my wrist. I got to get free to say goodbye to my Ol' Bird.

"Lee, what did I hear you just call me?"

"It's cool, Grandmama, I called you my Ol' Bird. I'm the only one who can call you that."

She grabbed her rolling pin and had it at my neck in one move. I didn't know she could move that fast. Flames were in her eyes with a dab of flour on her nose. I couldn't help laughing while she rebuked her nickname.

"I'm a hawk and I will hunt you down if I hear that name again, boy!"

The cold metal chair jolted me out of my recollection and back into his office. My mouth stuffed full of cloth to muffle my screaming. I started shaking and moving the chair, trying to break free of the ropes. Osbourne watched me after he ended his call. My tears were dripping on the rag that tied my mouth shut. The rope securing my legs bruised and burned my ankles each time I jolted myself, trying to break free. The chair moved back and forth, creating marks on the floor.

"You are messing up my floor. Stop moving, or I will stop you with a bullet," he said while studying his paperwork.

I gotta get to the hospital. But my urgency submitted to the fear of being shot. I don't remember when it happened or when he captured me. I'm not a man to get scared, but when my stomach turns, this ain't good.

A month ago, I had asked my boy Hardhead, (government name: Howard Stowe) about moving some crack around. I needed the cash to help my brother out paying for Grandmama's prescriptions. I wasn't sure why she was taking so many pills, but I knew that shit ain't cheap. The north side of St. Louis was too crowded with sellers. Hardhead suggested I move a party drug into the untapped market of the business district of Clayton, Missouri. Thousands of lawyers, stockbrokers, and the elite with rebellious, bored kids. Payday for me. Hardhead said Osbourne would be in touch, not the other way around. He also warned me to do my dirt and get out. "Don't linger around him. If you value your life, don't ask him about his name," he had said.

After that conversation, I ran into two of Osbourne's henchmen who handed me a backpack full of what I needed. Three hundred grams of powdered sugar. His price was about twelve hundred dollars and he'd said that whatever else I made was for me. Well, in this case, it was to help my brother out with the Ol' Bird and her mounting bills. They said Osbourne wants his money at the end of the month. "All his months have thirty days. Give the backpack with the unmarked cash in a separate Ziploc bag to the man with freckles at the corner of Delmar and Clayton."

Two weeks later, my dumbass brother found my stash and flushed it down the toilet. We had a good fight that day. I needed $500 to pay my loan off. I ended up getting enough cash out of Becky's when I robbed that joint. It had almost become a botched robbery when my partner Shawn slipped on the wet floor and broke his leg. He was trapped inside when the police showed up.

Hardhead was right about Osbourne finding me, but I gave him back his money. I handed the backpack to the only black dude with freckles on the street that night. It would be my luck if it was some random tourist I gifted with my hard-earned cash.

Osbourne was reading papers in a room only illuminated by the lamp on his dark chocolate-stained desk. I made out the shadows of three large bodyguards standing behind him, not making a sound. One of them was stationed near a closet, opening it up every so often. A fourth guard manned the entrance to his office. *He's an organized man*, I noted. The glare from his glasses reflected my terrified face when he peered at me.

"What are those marks on your arm?" he asked in a deep, calm, even voice. He sounded a lot like the black man on the insurance commercials.

"Tombstones," I said the best I could with a rag in my mouth.

"Tombstones? Do you kill someone and mark your body with a tombstone?" he inquired again, studying the artwork.

"Why am I here?" I asked.

"To learn some respect," he paused and continued reading his papers. *Fuck this. I got to get to the hospital.* Being in the room with her clawed at my mind. I tried wiggling my hands free when a red light on my chest convinced me to stop wiggling.

"Untie this man," he commanded without looking up.

One of his bodyguards walked behind me and untied me. The rope tightened on my arms, burning my skin as he yanked and shook it loose. My head jerked forward as he untied the rag. He then walked around and snatched it out of my mouth. He was the color of midnight with a short haircut, gigantic bug eyes, and about my height, but he weighed a good two hundred and twenty pounds.

"Do you know who I am?" Osbourne asked while the rope dropped from my wrists. I stayed seated and looked him in the eyes.

"I heard about you," I said.

"I run a clean ship. I have a big hat and bigger cattle. Understand?"

"Mr. Osbourne, I paid you back your money. Why am I here?"

"Good question, Mr. Brooks, one I already answered. To learn respect and math. You think I can't count. Miguel, can I count?" The shorter bodyguard walked over to the desk next to Osbourne's chair.

"Yes, you can, sir," Miguel smiled.

"Mr. Brooks seems to disagree. Right, Mr. Brooks?"

"What are you talking about?"

"What was our deal, Mr. Brooks?"

I stood up to leave when a force like a fifty-pound bag of cement landed on my shoulder. Out of my peripheral, one large hand pushed against my will to stand, and in the same motion, the barrel of a gun rested on my forehead. I sat back down.

"Kumal, why are you working so hard? Let him go." Kumal let go of my shoulder and stood behind me while Osbourne continued. "Mr. Brooks, standing next to me, is Miguel Cooper. He is one of my bodyguards. He likes his nickname, Mess, but I think Miguel is a distinguished name. The one with the short fuse who almost killed you is Kumal."

He didn't introduce the third one or say a word to him. Occasionally the nameless guard would check the closet door, come back, and stand silent.

"You wouldn't want to miss the excitement, would you?" he asked me with his eyes on his desk.

I flicked my wrist to check my watch that wasn't there. I looked at Osbourne, and he held up a bag. He turned it upside down and my gun, phone, wallet, and watch came dancing out like jacks on the sidewalk.

"I know every play you are going to play before you play it. You are pocket change—useless shit I keep around. I notice it frustrates you being here. Frustration unreleased is no good. I'll release your frustrations."

Grandmama's clock is ticking. I stood again to reach for my gun when three lights appeared on my forehead. I didn't stop this time. I grabbed my gun off his desk and swiveled until I had aimed the barrel at the middle of his head. He waved off his bodyguards.

"I said I don't have time."

"Mr. Brooks. Why don't you have a look out the window?"

I turned to face another building, and it was all dark except one floor illuminated with four red lasers pointing through the windows. Two of the red lights were on my chest, one on my zipper, and one right in the center of my forehead.

"Mr. Brooks, I'm renovating that complex. I plan to lease lofts and office space on twelve floors, except the one that has four red dots on you. I didn't get where I am by being stupid. My protection works in three shifts, and their jobs are to make pieces of shit out of you when you make sudden moves like reaching for your gun. They're currently aiming Barrett fifty caliber rifles zeroed at three hundred yards with a Léopold 4.5-mil dot scope attached. The snipers are all Army-trained Hawkeyes, hitting fifty out of fifty targets in their final combat training exam. One twitch of my index finger and they will shoot the plaque off your yellow teeth."

I wondered if I had shit my pants. Osbourne didn't look like he smelled anything. I puffed my chest out a little. Well, at least I did something, even though the sweat on my forehead gave a different opinion of the situation. I laid my gun back on his desk.

"Your gun was empty. I don't want fear, just respect. Not too much to ask for, is it? Sit your skinny ass down."

I sat down, the cold metal pressing against the back of my legs.

"Good. Now, what was our deal?"

"One thousand, two hundred, and fifty dollars in thirty days."

"What did you give me?"

"I gave you all your money. In three weeks. Counted that shit twice."

"That's not what I counted."

He motioned for the figure in the shadows, who went to the closet again and pulled out a bag. I couldn't identify his face behind the dark of the room. He brought the bookbag, reached in, and pulled out the Ziploc that kept Osbourne's cash separate from mine. When he appeared under the light, I recognized him as the guy who had taken my money. Light-skinned, portly man with freckles under his eyes.

"I gave it all to him," I confirmed.

"This man here?" I nodded to his question while Osbourne counted the cash again. He licked his thumb as each bill passed to the side on the desk. It reminded me of my teachers in school who would wet their thumb with their tongue to pass out graded homework.

"I counted $1,150. Where is the rest?" Osbourne asked.

"If you would have looked through my shit, you would have seen the receipt I made him sign. Ask him." I sighed, thanking god for Grandmama pestering to always get everything in writing.

"I did see the receipt," Osbourne said, and the bag landed with a thump as the bodyguard dropped it.

"Mr. Osbourne wait—I—" In a flash of black polyester, Mess hit him with the blunt end of a pistol. Kumal jumped in and repeatedly kicked and punched the freckled guard until he looked like ground beef.

“Have a seat next to Mr. Brooks.” Osbourne intoned, as Kumal sat the beaten guard in the metal folding chair next to me.

“Mr. Brooks, sitting next to you is Belvedere Evans, also known as Cookie. Mr. Evans doesn’t understand respect either. Cookie and I had a deal just like you and I did. Give me my money. I want all my money. Never test my patience like Cookie, who decided it was okay to short me one hundred dollars.”

I knew I had counted that shit twice before I sealed that Ziploc. I shivered like it was twenty degrees outside, but I got a sweat going. He took a beating over a hundred bucks?

“It’s not that big a deal. I can loan him that,” I said.

“No, you can’t. You got $3.32. We emptied your pockets already.” He nodded to his desk, refreshing my memory. “Cookie gave me your Ziploc bag. He thought it would be okay to treat his buddy with my cash. You know who his friend was, Mr. Brooks?”

I didn’t answer. Osbourne grabbed my gun off his desk and shot the bodyguard who stood by the door. He fell over the copier leaving a smear of blood on the Xerox machine. I flinched along with Mess, Kumal, and a crying Cookie. Osbourne looked impassively and kept talking.

"Respect, Mr. Brooks. But all is not lost with you. I like you. You stood up for yourself. I trust you."

I heard his shoes squeak on the floor as he walked over to me and slapped my cheek.

"Don't ever fuck me."

I started imagining the worst at the hospital. My heart broke as I pictured her lying in her bed.

"Excuse me one moment, Mr. Brooks. Could someone grab the housekeeper?"

Miguel held a walkie-talkie to his face and whispered in the mouthpiece. I kept my eyes straight on Osbourne, bewildered he'd just disposed of his bodyguard like he would a razor. My phone rang on his desk. I couldn't see the name on the caller ID, but I'd bet the farm it was Jonas. I know he was angry I wasn't there. A short while later an older black man opened the creaking door to Osbourne's office and sauntered in, pushing a yellow rolling bucket by the mop immersed in scalding water. He whistled as he stepped past the corpse of the bodyguard. A red bandanna hung off the back pocket of faded blue denim overalls and a matching denim cap hid the white hair on his head. Osbourne took off his glasses and held them by the temples. I noticed he even had on charcoal dress socks to match his dark charcoal Stacy Adams shoes.

"Adrian, how are you?"

"Fine, sir, and you?" he replied with a rusty voice.

"Adrian, this is Mr. Brooks. Mr. Brooks, Adrian Cross." We both nodded. Osbourne patted him on the shoulder.

"How long have I known you? Twenty-plus years?"

"Yes sir, you helped me out a lot. I owe you everything. You are an honorable man," Adrian smiled.

"I leaned against my desk and my pants are dirty. Why?"

"I must have missed a spot, sir."

"You like seeing me dirty?"

"No, sir. I'm sorry," he pulled out a rag and wiped the desk.

"No worries." Osbourne twitched his extended index finger and a shot fired through the window, hitting Adrian in the left lower shoulder blade. Blood squirted out of his shirt where his heart stopped pumping. He fell over on the ground in front of me. A pool of blood appeared around his body. Osbourne hadn't been kidding about those sharpshooters.

"Get this piece of shit out of my office. NOW!"

Mess and Kumal picked up Adrian, one by the shoulders, and the other by the feet. The old man was heavy, so they struggled as they removed him. Osbourne walked back over in front of me and leaned against his now-clean desk, folding his arms. Cookie cried louder. I felt more sweat around my forehead and armpits.

"Know anyone in the cleaning business? I'm hiring," Osbourne asked, rolling his eyes, then continued. "Why are you selling drugs, Mr. Brooks?"

"To help my brother. To help my grandmother. We maxed out a credit card paying for her prescriptions," I sniffled, fighting back tears. "My Ol' Bird was rushed to the hospital a few weeks ago."

"Old bird? What's an old bird?"

"My grandma."

Osbourne sat back on the edge of his desk, leaned over, and got in my face.

"Don't you ever call her an old bird again. Do you know that's why I let your sorry ass even sell for me? Your grandmother, Miss Charon Mines, was my elementary school teacher. She saved my life. If you disrespect her again, I will fire so many bullets in your narrow ass that it will look like a woodpecker apartment complex. Our school didn't have a pot to piss in. We studied with leaking ceilings in our classrooms, and air conditioners that didn't work and no one would repair. Water dripped on our books, smearing the ink. I have my fourth-grade history book in my desk as a reminder of the bullshit they called going to school. We used the old textbooks the richer schools discarded. We learned with their trash. They paid her nickels to teach that class. She did it despite the money because she cared about us. She told us to be somebody, Mr. Brooks. I made a vow in her class to be a motherfucker. Here I am. This is only a start. We are better than selling drugs, Mr. Brooks. I will make things better for young men coming up like yourself, so we don't have to do this shit anymore. I'm running for office and I plan to change this shit. From the voting zones to the displacement of tax dollars. Everyone should have a fair start in life. You—You forgot your roots. Despite the odds against a black woman, your grandmother raised your ungrateful ass in that misery, and the respect she gets is 'an old bird'? I should beat the living shit out of you." He smiled.

"Excuse me one more moment, Mr. Brooks"

He pointed my gun at Cookie's face and blew his head across the room into a million pieces like cookie crumbs. I flinched as most of the red and pink splatter landed on the right side of my face and shoulders. He turned back to me, sniffing.

"The restroom is on the way out. Clean yourself up. I respect your intentions. We should do business again. You proved yourself today. I'm looking for men on my team I can trust. I owe your grandmother everything, and I'd like to give you an opportunity to work with me. Take some time and think about it. I will be in touch."

Today

"See, man, that's your problem. I wouldn't put up with that shit," I said as I put my shoe in the chair cushion to tie it.

"Lee, what would you have done?"

"Man, look. I would've—" After I finished tying my new Nikes with one leg on the kitchen chair, I sat down. I had tried to tell my older brother, Jonas, how to run game on these women. This dude walked in on his wife—or ex-wife—sleeping with his old neighbor, Hunter, last year. I almost shit myself laughing when he said he pulled a gun out and shot at the wall three times. Then he said Hunter peed on his sheets when he shot near his head. I laughed because I would have shot him too. My big bro put his foot down, but then he moved out of the house. Stupid ass. I would have put my foot right up her ass and tossed all her shit. Now he's working things out with her. Stupid ass. After going through all that, I wouldn't have nothing to do with it. He's too nice.

Then Neru had to move in next door. Neru Khudjan can make a hippie look like a violent extremist. He wore twelve thick dreadlocks on his head attached to a body drafted by the Denver Nuggets in the first round. Instead of shooting baskets, he'd rather shoot nouns and verbs. A poet who delivers daily and neither rain, nor snow, nor gloom of night will stay this moron from getting on my nerves. Peace this and peace that. There is a bullet from my piece right for his peaceful ass. When he gets together with Jonas, they talk about absolutely nothing. Neru is all about how we should love our women because the fabric of the black family is deteriorating. You can go to hell with some *fiber* of black families. His wife, Simi, is just as bad.

I left the drug game because of Grandmama and only because of Grandmama. On her deathbed, she gave Jonas all props and reassured him of how much of a man he had become. She got to me and all she said was I was hardheaded just like my daddy. I said, "Yes, I am, and what are you going to do about it?" She smiled and asked me to be a man and stop all that shit.

"You know better don'cha boy."

My stupid ass had agreed with a smile. Yeah, seeing my grandmama in a hospital changed my mind, and I'd promised to act right.

"Are you listening?" I interrupted myself, noticing Jonas staring at our family picture in the hallway.

"Are you asking for a fight?" he replied.

"Fight? You can't even hit your cheatin' ass wife from five feet away."

Yeah, I hit the sweet spot. He hates it when I bring up his ex-wife's affair and how he was too chicken shit to pull the trigger when he caught her in the act. The microwave cooked my cuisine for the evening—two Salisbury steaks, mashed potatoes, and corn on the cob. It's not like Grandmama used to cook, but not bad for three bucks. After it beeped, I got up from the table for my meal while Jonas poured another Coke. I saw his eyebrows close in together to make him frown.

"Don't be getting all pissed. We still family," I said.

"Family, my ass. I had a bad day already, and here you go."

"I told you once, and I'll keep on telling you, you're too damn nice. The difference between me and you is..."

"What?"

"I wouldn't have missed."

He slammed his cup down as if that intimidated me. Wrong answer, bro. I countered with slamming the microwave door after grabbing dinner.

"And you went back like a punk." I continued.

"Look, man, until you walk in my shoes—"

"Shoes nothing. I would have plugged the bitch."

He stayed silent while sipping his Coke. I didn't care. She messed with family when she cheated. Jonas is a good man. He always keeps a job—two for the fun of it. Some days money was tight, but he always talked about giving her roses and shit. She didn't deserve shit. Then his stupid ass got all whipped, and here she decided to play around. I would have more respect for her if she'd have told him straight up. Why did he go back? I never read a book twice because the ending doesn't change.

My dinner started burning my hand, so I pushed about three weeks of paper plates, old TV dinners, and shit to the side of the table, then set it down before I burnt my fingers. Jo got up and pulled a frozen pizza out the freezer, unwrapped it, and pushed a few buttons on the screen, starting the hum of the microwave again. Jonas shoving more shit off the kitchen table interrupted the silence.

"Damn, Lee. When you gon' clean up?"

"I ain't the only one that live here, am I?"

"Grandmama wouldn't tolerate your sloppy ass."

"My gun is ready for her too. May she rest her praising the Lord ass in peace. I hated that shit, getting up at five in the morning for church. I'm like damn the service don't start until the reverend wants to show up."

"What time was that? About ten til' twelve and the bulletin said 10:00 a.m. sharp," he said, smiling. I imagined Grandmama rolling in her grave.

"True, and then what? Every weekend is revival, which means six more hours of watching these morons break floorboards screaming and jumping like they got shot in the ass."

He pulled his steaming pizza out, grinning.

"Which means it's already 8:00 a.m. Monday morning and time for school. Ain't nobody done no homework, sitting in church since the cock crowed. Then Grandmama wants to put us on punishment like it's our fault."

He smacked my hand when I tried getting a piece of his pizza. Then I got quiet because I had to break the news to him. He's the calmer out of the two of us, but I've seen him fly off the chain a couple of times. Like when he tried to put a spark in his own wife. What I had to tell him now might be one of those times.

I speared my steak, ready to take down another chunk when the memory of that wheel spinning over my head flooded into my mind. I still couldn't believe how we came out with no scratches after the car rolled in that ditch all those years ago. I woke up many nights on a soaked pillow, reaching for my parents only to find my cold steel next to me. I can hear Grandmama's sobbing as the court proceedings looped like a terrible song stuck in my mind.

Rogan Stone had been out drinking with his boys when he drove home intoxicated. He was with his best friend, and several cops confirmed they were popping brews in the car. Well, he didn't see the stop sign, stopping our lives. By the time Pop seen him, it was too late. The force from colliding with a car going sixty miles per hour in a forty-mile-per-hour zone flipped our sedan five times, killing my mom and dad in the front seat. Rogan Stone ended up getting twenty years for each of my parents for manslaughter and felony DWI.

Well hell, now is as good a time as ever. I dug the front page of the day's news off a messy floor of shoes, credit card applications, a mop, a broom, and an empty box of chicken fried rice next to my chair. I threw it at my brother and kept eating.

"What's up?" he asked with a mouthful of pepperoni and cheese.

"Read it."

He was taking all day, so I told him the gist of the article.

"Rogan Stone got released today."

"I thought he got twenty years for each—"

"Good behavior. He got out on good behavior."

Jonas skimmed the article.

"He impressed a parole board, huh? I'm not impressed."

"Me neither."

He continued reading in silence. This didn't make any sense. Rogan was that well-behaved he qualified for early release for killing our parents? That's a bunch of bullshit. What I didn't tell Jonas was I already got the scoop on where Rogan lives and where he plans to work. I'd had a taste for my favorite scrambled omelet with Mexican rice, chorizo, beans, and con-queso one night, so I'd gone to the Waffle Diner. My friend

Della, who works there, told me the manager told her after work that the owner read about Rogan's story and decided to help him get back on his feet. That motherfucker walked out of jail and had a job waiting on him. What a feel-good story. I don't know if Jo has moved on with his life, but I will celebrate my own feel-good story when I end Rogan's.

I ran my hand down the two tombstone tattoos on my arm—one for each of my parents he killed. Each tombstone had my parents' initials and birth dates scribbled inside, and the tattoos descended from my arm like tears. My finger ran across the smooth surface of my skin where I planned a third one in memory of the unexpected death of Mr. Rogan Stone.

"I struggle to understand this system," Jonas said, looking away.

"I want a new tattoo," I replied, spearing another piece of steak.

After eating, Jonas started cleaning off the table, placing paper plates and old mail in the trash. He crushed a few soda cans with his bare hands for recycling. I figured he was angry enough about the news, so I debated letting him in on my plan. He remained quiet while cleaning, muttering "pigsty" every so often. He kept the newspaper under his arm when he left an hour later.

Goddamn.

Scramble

I walked outside into a mouthful. Neru was standing on the porch, as usual, waiting for his kids to arrive home. I'm about sick of his ass.

"Hey, Lee, pull your pants up. No one wants to see your underwear." He reminded me of the cartoon character Ned Flanders, Homer Simpson's bothersome-ass neighbor, but with the Koran and three-foot dreads running down his dark-skinned back. I could never make it to my car parked on the curb without him saying shit.

"Hey, man, my kids don't want to see your Superman briefs. You think that's hard? You think that's gangsta? Don't that mean something else? Didn't that start in jail, young blood?"

"Man, it means I'm about to—" I looked at his kids coming up the steps. "Man, it's just my clothes."

His son ran under him for a good-afternoon hug.

"Gangsta Lee, come here for a minute. I want to talk to you."

"Man, I gotta make a run. I'll get at you later."

I had nowhere to go except away from him. I needed an excuse and couldn't think of one. Damn.

"Hey, buddy, school is over. Why didn't you wake up and run to school? How can gangstas run with sagging pants? Are you too gangsta for school, young blood?"

Man, if he called me young blood one more time there would be blood on the walk to his house. I smiled and kept on going.

"I'll get with you tomorrow."

"I just talked with your brother."

I turned back. My brother always spilled his guts. Jonas can't keep shit to himself. Bitch ass. I gave in and walked back to him.

"Lee, I heard what happened."

"And?"

"And? How do you feel?"

"Like shit."

"Listen, I'm here for you, man. We got to stick together. The man got it set up to make us fail. If that was us, man, then, man, we'd be in the electric chair, man."

How many "mans" can he say in a damn sentence? I spaced out while Neru continued on about life being unfair. He ain't gotta worry about this one. I will serve justice. Mr. Stone will be sentenced to solitary confinement six feet underground in a casket.

"Lee, are you listening?"

"Huh?"

"You ain't listened to a single word I said. Why can't you act like your brother?"

"Maybe he needs to act like me."

"That's the problem with these young bloods. All that damn rap crap got your head clogged up."

"Man, you were listening to Az-Zhan in your car this morning," I said.

"What? Not me, man. It must have been my kids." Neru looked away for a moment, tongue-tied.

I scoffed, knowing for a fact I'd heard his trunk rattling earlier from the bass of one of the dead rapper's songs.

"Gangsta blood, pull up ya pants."

"Man, why you always coming with that bullshit?" I stepped close to the edge of the wet grass Neru must have watered earlier. I hate cleaning my shoes.

"Man, no woman wants a no-good man. They want a clean brother like me." He popped his collar like he got swagger.

"Please."

"G-Money, what is the plan with your life? You need a job." I thought he exhaled fertilizer as his words hit me. Phew.

"Call me Lee."

"Speak English, Lee. Half the time I can't understand what you are saying," he said.

I stared off into space.

"Do you need help with a résumé? Have you filled out any job applications? I can get you some."

"Jobs ain't paying shit."

"Don't say that. There are plenty of opportunities out there. You gotta find them. Now, what's the plan?"

"The plan is to get paid," I said holding up my phone. "Opportunity's ringing."

I turned and walked off. I had enough of him for the day. There wasn't no goddamn phone ringing. I swear my ears were bleeding from his non-stop talking. I decided to go to the gym to use my anger to move some weight.

Chapter 4

Dr. Watson

I needed to lose a few pounds and burn off some frustration. Afternoon workouts are great for proper stress management. Since healthcare is becoming expensive, I added thirty to forty-five minutes of high-intensity cardio during my lunch hour. I've read great reviews about this new fitness center. With its proximity to work, I can incorporate training into my daily routine.

"Hey Dr. Watson, what's up?"

Unfortunately for Le'Angelo Brooks, I was walking to the entrance to the gym when I ran into my former student. Room four, row three, seat facing the wall next to the coat rack. Five reported incidents of fistfights with Howard Stowe, Bachari Hades, Walter McKinney, Darrel Montgomery, and Jim Paulson, which was a knockout in the bathroom. Plus he lost a tooth to Belinda Bryans. He was the opposite of his older brother, who excelled academically. I noticed him on one knee tying his shoes as I approached.

"Le'Angelo Brooks. How are you, young man?"

"Good. Just coming out the gym. That's what's up. I haven't seen you in a long time."

He smiled as he adjusted his gym bag on his shoulder to fist bump me, which I returned. Le'Angelo excelled in English and can comprehend average multiplication and division problems. I will use a conversion quiz from the lesson plan executed on October 9th, 1994. Challenge initiated.

"It's been fifteen years. What are you doing with yourself?" I asked.

"Right now, I'm trying to find a job, you know. It's hard out here."

"What about college? Are you enrolled?"

I surveyed the building. No cameras. Parking lot full, but everyone is inside. The landscaping crew is busy working behind the grounds, out of sight.

"Damn, my neighbor just said the same thing about college and shit. But naw, I ain't got that kind of cash on me yet. I want to save up and enroll soon. Besides money, I'm still not sure what I want to do for a career."

"'Damn,' Mr. Brooks?"

"Oh, I'm sorry."

"Le'Angelo, maximize your opportunities from financial aid and scholarships. You have plenty of time to figure out a path that will be not only financially stable but will fulfill you and provide you with a sense of meaning. Also, consider trade schools." I took a breath and changed topics. "Well, I was just heading in to tour the facility and maybe sign up. How is it in there?"

"Not too bad. It's a gym. Ain't nothing new to see."

"Lee."

I lowered my head and made eye contact as my glasses almost slid down my nose. He's trying me already. After all these years, he continues to employ the word "ain't" and double negatives despite losing his recess twice.

"Sorry, there isn't anything new, but it's pretty clean in there. Lots of free weights and cardio machines."

"There's nothing free about $49.95 per month, is there?"

"Damn straight."

"Lee?"

"Sorry, my bad. Well, good to see you."

"Hold on. I need some help starting out. You look like you are in good shape. Can you give me a few pointers?"

"Aww man, I just bench press you know, and do some curls for the girls."

I smiled.

“What about your legs?” I inquired.

“Man, please, these things are pencil sticks, but I can run like no tomorrow. Wanna race?” He asked, punching my arm. Too bad I don’t want to play.

“True, you have lean muscle,” I said, grabbing a piece of my midsection. “You better appreciate it while you can.”

“That’s what’s up, but hey, I gotta get—”

“Wait, how much should I start with?” I interrupted his escape plan.

One more look around and still no witnesses. I hope he’s prepared. He began reaching in his bag for his phone. But I don’t think he will need it. Ever.

“Oh, that’s easy. Lightweight first, then work your way up so you don’t get injured.”

“C’mon, I need more information than that.”

“What you do need?”

“I’m working chest today if I get time. How much weight should I start with on the bench press?”

“I’m not too sure. You are bigger than I am and I’m benching one hundred and sixty five pounds for twelve reps. I had to work for that.”

“Whoa, you are pretty strong there. So, what is that on the bar?”

“A forty-five and a ten on each side of the barbell.”

"Now, I'm new to the gym lingo. That's forty-five pounds and a ten-pound weight on each side. Perfectly balanced, right?"

"Yeah, if you tip the bar over then I'll laugh at you," he said.

His facial features are cartoonish. Time has grown his hair out and eleven cornrows race to the back of his head. His giant nostrils sit under Bambi eyes. Too bad there will be a bullet in between them because of his lack of comprehension.

"I'm used to watching international lifting events. You ever watch one?" I asked.

"Yeah, they can move some serious weight."

"Funny thing is, they use the metric system. That's confusing me; I'm so used to hearing the metric standards verses the imperial standards for measurements. Your max bench? How much would that be in kilograms?" I pressed.

"Damn, that's funny, I see the kilos on the weight all the time and I don't pay any attention."

"You don't know, Lee?"

"Off the top of my head, I can't remember."

"Think."

"I gotta get going," he answered.

"Aren't you going to help me?" I asked, as my smile dissipated. My patience is reaching the last rep. Failure eminent.

"I told you, I can't remember," he said as his nostrils flared just like they use to right before he got into a fight.

"Lee, we are wasting time. Now, please advise me how to convert pounds into kilograms."

"Hold up Doc, why are you getting so mad?"

"I'm losing my patience with you."

I've always hated being called Doc, and I certainly can't stand it being uttered from an idiot. Lee looked away, dumbfounded. He stared at the ground, waiting for an answer to appear. Had he listened years ago, it might have.

I reached for my gun in my pocket and began rubbing the barrel. I can't wait any longer.

"Le'Angelo Brooks, Class of 1994, I demand to know how you convert 165 pounds to kilograms. Can you help me?"

"Pardon me, sir, it's quite simple, one pound is 0.45 kilograms. They chisel both metric and American conversions into the mold. Forty-five pounds is twenty kilograms, the twenty-five-pound weights are eleven kilograms, and so on. The calculations are off by a few decimal places, but it's enough for a great approximation," I heard from behind me.

"That's what's up. See, there you go, Doc. It was great seeing you. Take care."

My intention to blow his inoperable brain out his skull with a bullet ruined. Challenge interrupted.

He should play the lottery today. The lucky Le'Angelo walked away, and I turned to face a smiling man dressed in a black Polo shirt with an orange Bargain Box logo on the chest pocket. I released my gun, found a sharp edge on my office keys, and rubbed the jagged edge until I broke skin. Now I wanted to end the life of this young man for blurting out the correct answer, interrupting my test.

"Hi, I didn't mean to butt in. You're Dr. Watson, I presume."

"I presume you cheated."

"Excuse me?"

"Nice to meet you," I said, reaching out my hand with a small trail of blood. I said nothing further about his unwelcomed disruption as my attention shifted to more important matters inside. I made a mental note to find and re-challenge Mr. Brooks at a future time.

Moments Later

"Sir, over here we have the swimming pool. Swimming is a great cardio workout and it's easy on the joints."

"I agree. I have to be conscious of the old knees at my age, young man," I said, continuing the tour of the gym with the freckled-faced attendant hell-bent on selling me a membership.

I'd debated killing him outside after he interrupted my challenge of Lee. He is lucky I didn't shoot both him and my former student.

Bargain Box just opened a few months ago. It looks nice, but I remembered nothing he told me. As well as adding some fitness to my lunchtime, I'd heard that Osbourne's bodyguards train here and I had to see for myself. We continued walking while I debated the uselessness of physical exertion beyond an aerobic workout. Anything past one hundred and twenty beats per minute of the heart does more harm than good.

"Over here, sir, is the daycare. Our daycare hours are Monday through Friday from eight to five."

"I see."

We continued walking while I noted the giant men and women lifting heavy weights, yelling loud enough to let everyone know it. They paled compared to an ant. One of the smallest creatures yet the most organized and strongest, lifting and moving over ten times their body weight in silence. Working with diligence in the summer to prepare for the winter ahead. In stride with the mighty ant, I also store my accounts until the time arrives that I cannot work with such a drive.

"Sir?"

"Excuse me?"

"I asked if it will be a single or joint membership. We have a special going on until the end of the month," the attendant stated, rubbing his ginger hair as we walked past the cardio theater.

"It's just me."

"We give cash back for any friends and family you refer to Bargain Box Gym."

Well, I do have one associate. A government-ordered directive had hired the two of us to kill the matriarch of a mob family in witness protection many years ago. Going by the nickname "Vegas," Victor Goodson is a gamble on whether he gets the job done. The agent of chance's latest assignment didn't go so well, which is why I'm here to finish the job. Victor's mission: knock off Osbourne, who had announced his entry into the political arena by running for state representative. He is also one of the area's biggest crime bosses, having a hand in over sixty percent of the gun and drug trafficking market in St. Louis. No crimes are ever traced back to him because either the person arrested doesn't say a word or they end up dead. Osbourne has put his hands into the methamphetamine game and is now reaping the benefits of addicts in the city's surrounding counties. According to my informant, Victor's job was never completed, and he's since disappeared.

Scramble

I identified my current target bent over the drinking fountain.

My informant had inquired about my mental state prior to sharing the intel of Osbourne's associates who frequent this establishment. And for good reason. My last chance at sanity had passed away with my wife when the doctor diagnosed her with stage four cancer. The cancer crept into her lymph nodes like a burglar in the shadows of a hallway at night. The fight was long and she'd suffered hard. Many nights, I'd have rather worked long hours at the school than sit and witness my wife succumb to the merciless torture of cancer. We'd celebrated triumphantly with hugs and kisses when she beat it the first time, although it cost her the flowing locks that draped her shoulders. The second bout of cancer beat her in a landslide victory when it came out of remission a year later. Cancer is the unstoppable clock, a countdown to the end of your life, and the ticks of my insanity replaced the anger, frustration, and sadness of losing my wife. I also lost her name and I dare not recall it. I forget all their names lest I endure the ferocity of the memories escaping that opened door.

Alongside my passion to kill lies a passion to arm the youth with knowledge. Soon they will no longer be on-deck in the struggles of life; they will face the pitcher themselves. My job is to weed out the useless and train the ones who can excel. If the doctor had known more, maybe he could have saved her life.

We sat down at the attendant's desk after finishing the tour. I signed half of my name on the dotted line to seal our one-year, month-to-month contract when I paused.

"Mind if I check out the locker rooms first?"

"Oh yeah, I forgot." He stood to come with me but I cut him off.

"No tour guide needed. I also must use the restroom. Give me five minutes and I'll be right back to sign."

I entered the tan-colored dressing room, a few minutes after my target. I congratulated a lifter on his good depth from an earlier 226-kilogram squat for ten repetitions. When he left, and the room was clear, I crept along the side of the wall. Right before I sat down to sign the contract, I had observed my next project stepping into this room. The victim was currently belting out a song by Usher as he washed his face. *He can carry a tune with such a robust tenor voice—he would have excelled in opera. He shows good vocal range on the top notes. A sad waste of talent.* Ninety seconds passed. Distance equals six meters. My moves were quick, calculated, and without a sound.

I had on a bluish-gray trench coat covering dark pants and a sky blue and green checkerboard necktie. I always dress for the kill. It's kind of like a joining of the victim's life and my zest for death in holy matrimony. Fifty-three seconds passed. My trench brushed the lockers behind me as I passed the members' storage space at a snail's pace. No drama, just the math:

1) Victim appears to be five-six or five-seven, muscular build—say 188 pounds with nine percent body fat.

2) Victim is washing hands and flexing in front of a mirror. Arms engorged with blood, concluding strength conditioning on the upper body.

3) Lower lumbar appears out of line by six degrees to the left and lower; approximately five degrees from the right and upper.

4) Legs smaller and less mature than upper body muscles. No known core strength. The chance for resistance? Thirty-three percent—minimum. Threat for attack downgraded.

5) Victim named Miguel Cooper, also known as Mess.

6) Victim occupation: head of security for Osbourne.

7) Fighting skills: expert in Tai Chi and Judo.

Distance equals half a meter.

I crept over to his left while he scrubbed his face in the mirror. My shoulder in the trench coat appeared next to his bewildered reflection just in time for him to see a quarter-inch barrel that held three super-cooled liquid hydroxide darts sharpened by a titanium blade pointed down one inch below his chin.

"Open wide," I said. His shaking mouth swallowed the barrel of the pistol. I pushed him down to his knees.

Zero seconds passed.

"You're dead, so don't think about moving."

He kneeled speechless, clearly wondering what he smoked, drank, or injected to imagine this, so I proceeded.

"I use this gun for special occasions. By the time your brain fires a signal through your dendrites and synapses ordering you to move, I will have fired a 0.75-inch diameter hydroxide dart created in a vacuum chamber thirty degrees below zero sharpened by 0.01 tolerance titanium into your neck. It will puncture your bronchial tube en route to your spinal column. Once it hits your spine, the chasm between vertebrae you have created by looking up at me will offer no resistance, traversing your entire spinal cord, severing the branch nerves to every functioning part of your body, including your vital organs. It will then exit after ripping through your bowels, landing on the floor where it will melt away due to the excessive pressure from the exit wound in 0.84 seconds. You, my friend, will stand there and witness your body shutting down. Your last memory will be the sensation of warmth from the feces that will fill your underwear as you lose control of your sphincter muscle. I'm killing Osbourne, and you are in my way."

On second thought, I pulled the gun out of his mouth. A coat of saliva glossed the tip. I hear voices outside the hallway getting closer. I slipped my dart gun in the pocket of my trench, and unholstered my 9mm with a CGS Mod 9 suppressor.

Scramble

"I'll give you one chance to live. You have five seconds to answer my question."

"B-B-B-B-B-But—"

The silencer attached to my gun made a *peeewwt* sound as one thin blood trail descended his neck. His eyes remained open and his jaw locked shut as our wedding together concluded in a nasty divorce. I didn't have a chance to challenge his math skills, and I didn't have time to wait for him to enunciate a response. He fell over the sink and hit his head on the faucet as I jumped down and checked his pulse. Five, four, three, two, one… His heart stopped beating. I needed to get back to work. I pulled his head up, then dropped it back on the sink as I heard it thud. I turned off the running water. Such a waste of resources. I measured the size of the lockers. Depth? Sustainable. Height? Can accommodate with a few adjustments.

I used a towel nearby to wrap his bleeding head. After I checked the sink for blood, I lowered Miguel to the ground. The door creaked. An older gentleman walked in and headed to the sink next to the one Miguel had used. I stretched his arms like wings, then extended the left leg towards his head, twisting my body so it blocked the man's view of the corpse and the blood pool near his mouth.

"Miguel, relax. Sit still while I stretch you out," I said loud enough for the man to hear. "Quit moving, or you will make it worse."

"Is he okay?"

The elderly man tried peering over. I turned to face him holding Miguel's leg.

"Sir, he's fine, just a cramp, you know."

"Yeah, a good ol' charley horse. He needs to take a salt bath when he gets home," he said as he applied deodorant to his armpits after removing his wet t-shirt.

"I agree, and a reminder to eat more potassium from tomatoes or bananas before a strenuous workout," I responded. "Daily massages at my rates may get a bit too expensive."

No one laughed. I began moving his leg back and forth as Miguel laid still. The older man got his belongings, shut the door to his large locker, then left. I wasn't sure if muscle stimulation decreased flaccidity. I brought both knees to his chin and lifted Miguel into the locker the old man had used. After a few hard pushes, the body yielded. I pushed the door shut and secured the latch. Then I called the tailor again and gave him my measurements. I told him to look for the body in a day or two. He obliged and tried again to arrange an appointment to chat. After I blew him off, I finished signing on the dotted line of the contract to the delight of the attendant, making sure I paid extra for a full-size locker rental. Once the demand for locker number fifty-seven was agreed upon, I hurried to the car to retrieve a key lock. The tailor should have no difficulties finding him. Killing the bodyguard checked off one item on my to-do list. Next: Osbourne.

Chapter 5

Dr. Watson

"Miss Colwell, this morning your actions toward Ms. Minnow were unacceptable. We need to stand as a single united front with the parents as we educate these kids. Witnessing the child's acceptance of punishment is part of the job."

"Dr. Watson, that is abuse. Period," Miss Colwell replied.

She sat across from me in my office as I held my nine-millimeter in my lap. The desk hid my legs below the wood grain finish. I stroked the metal surface of the barrel like a sleeping cat.

"I'm sorry if you can't stomach real discipline," I said.

"I'm sorry, you must be crazy if you think I'm going to sit here and let that woman beat that child like an animal." I frowned at her retort, growing restless with Miss Colwell.

"Punishment for excess is poverty of the mind, while scarcity flourishes in despondence. I will converse with Isaiah and let him know the magnitude of the struggle, and how his actions now will affect his future later. We have enough men calling our own women bitches. Don't you agree?"

"Well yes, that is why I called his mom."

"I think Isaiah learned his lesson. Don't you agree?"

I placed my finger right along the trigger as I imagined a red spot on Miss Colwell's forehead leaking with blood from one squeeze. Truth and non-violence are as old as the hills. Maybe some tough love from these parents would create a curiosity to exchange facts and information instead of punches. If these kids were aware of the consequences of their actions, they would think before they act. I will teach them the consequences of ignorance. Each day allows me another chance. With my free hand, I fingered my mouse, clicking on a new e-mail that just arrived.

"Sir, is there anything else you need?" Miss Colwell stood to leave.

"I'm not finished with you. Sit down."

Always in a rush to leave; she'd only been here for forty minutes. Just like she'd been the first student ready to go home from school. Backpack filled with books, jacket on, but there was still fifteen minutes left. Room nine, seat three, row two. I coughed to hide the noise of the clip locking in place.

That's where it originates. Disrespect is in style.

I looked at Miss Colwell, who was looking at her phone.

"Miss Colwell, I'm losing my patience with you. Can you sit still for just a moment?" Back then, she wore a yellow bow in her hair. I remember disciplining her for packing up her belongings with ten minutes left in the day. Distance equals one meter.

"Dr. Watson, with all due respect, it's been five minutes and you haven't said one word to me."

"Well, let me start with a question."

"Dr. Watson, your conference call with Dr. Gasen begins in five minutes," Arissa Hall, my administrative assistant, said after she poked her head in the office. She bears a striking resemblance to Diana Ross in the seventies. I love the different hairstyles Arissa wears, regularly changing from a short afro to natural twists and everything in between. She nodded at Miss Colwell.

"Thank you, Arissa. Miss Colwell, we will pick up this discussion at a later time. You may leave." Miss Colwell shook her head as she left. She should be thankful I didn't challenge her knowledge of basic trigonometry.

Conference calls: the shared experience of people who do not want to see each other. At the same time technology has brought the world together, we have put distance between ourselves. After I dialed in and entered the passcode, I listened with eyes closed, my mind on other things. The district superintendent rambled on about test scores, uniform dress codes, and accreditation. Dr. Stanford Gasen is an eloquent speaker, but his words were full of emptiness and preoccupied with political correctness as he sought transition from the local schools to a seat in the government. The future council member had one opponent: my next target, Osbourne. The man with St. Louis in his wallet.

Dr. Gasen, like Osbourne, spoke with reporters and news conferences in mind. Reporters bombarded him with questions and his comebacks were in the form of graceful ice-skating around each issue. He didn't realize how thin the ice was and I hoped, for his sake, he didn't fall in. The water's freezing; no one will be around to pull him out.

In closed-door meetings, we both agreed Osbourne was a horrible fit for office—the worst possibility for election. Dr. Conant Xavier, a professor at Happy Canyon Community College, said change begins with a single step forward. Where Dr. Xavier erred is that change sometimes begins with a step backward too. Peace does not mean quiet. That was my role. I would step backward and snuff out Osbourne's life, ending his chance for election. I would look him in his eyes as he vanished, leaving nothing to view but a corpse.

"Watson."

I hit the unmute button on my phone and answered. “Go ahead, Stanford.”

“We have to stay in the upper half of the Missouri School Certification test scores. We will leave behind no child. Presented with the many challenges of trying to meet a ninety percent success rate, how will you handle these challenges for your team?”

I sat up in my chair and prepared myself. My gun slid off my lap. I leaned over to pick it up and nestled it back in place.

“Stanford, I’m sorry to say the success rate is commensurate to at-home engagement with the curriculum. We can only present the material to the students. Home life plays a significant role in our students’ academic success, as our influence is restricted to school environments. Economic factors are involved, as the parent—I’m referring to both single parents and married—works to support the household. The parents’ obligation is to communicate the responsibility of the student to grasp the material and not to present roadblocks to the teacher. Challenging these inhibitors is what will propel the student to success.”

I let it soak in, then continued.

“We do, however, have control over the environment in which we present the material. It isn’t what the child retains, but the learning atmosphere that hurts us on the Missouri

Certification. Can the child recite what he knows in the form of a test, or is he sitting so uncomfortably in his chair that he's distracted? Is the child too cold to stay focused? We need to push initiatives to update our schools to at least the standards in the surrounding counties. Why do our kids have to learn in such dilapidated buildings? We need recent books current on the facts. Pluto isn't a planet anymore. Do the kids know that? Internet access is needed to challenge the myths presented in our older textbooks."

I paused once more to whet the palate. Arissa walked in again and signaled someone was there to see me. I gestured, "In a minute."

"We are also challenged with the media's perception of success. Current culture downplays the importance of education by luring youth into believing that improper dress, grammar, and lewd conduct will reap a financial harvest."

Stanford interrupted. "So, blame the parents and the TV. Protest our local TV stations and push for the internet. I can see the amount of suspensions due to accessing pornographic websites on the rise, Watson."

He chuckled, but I didn't entertain his joke. I put my finger on the trigger of my gun. I wished Arissa was not here today.

"I have someone outside my office. I will call you back to finish."

"Don't forget, because I have to talk to you about an offer presented to Happy Canyon. Read the email I just sent you."

"Will do."

It relieved me to end the call. How dare he joke about the condition of our schools? I felt the grip on my gun tighten, thinking of his incredulous mockery of my students' learning environment. I placed the gun in the drawer under my desk. I take my responsibility for the next generation seriously. I felt a little nauseous, standing up to greet my mystery guest, whom I guessed was a parent requesting an early pickup of a child. I clenched my teeth and my fist when I opened the office door and was greeted by the Republican candidate for the alderman in the Sixth Ward, Osbourne. I tried to put forth sincerity, but my brows suggested otherwise. I pushed my oval glasses back to the top of my nose.

"Mr. Osbourne, welcome to Happy Canyon Elementary. How may I help you?"

I signaled for Arissa to bring Osbourne some coffee. Hopefully laced with arsenic.

"Clark, it's been a long time since we have seen each other, hasn't it? Such sweet sorrow."

I raised my eyebrow. Romeo and Juliet?

"Call me Dr. Watson, please." I repeated myself, "How may I help you?"

"Clark, I'm here to help *you.* I'm here to influence the education of these adolescent minds."

I counted only two unarmed bodyguards with him, who stood outside the door wearing black polo shirts tucked into dress pants. I chuckled because I was the reason he was short-staffed.

"I would like to donate one hundred tablets to Happy Canyon. I also have an appointment with the broadband company to discuss the installation of high-speed internet. They are outside now."

Arissa's smile of gratitude for his act of generosity turned to surprise when I declined his offer. Osbourne's attempt to shine a media spotlight on himself did not fly over my head.

"I will not accept any gift from dirty money."

"Yes, you will. These kids deserve an equal chance to compete with the well-funded rural educational establishments."

"I will not accept any gift from money earned at the expense of a drug addiction."

"Dr. Watson, wouldn't your supervisor, Dr. Gasen, frown at the thought of you turning down a chance to impact the upcoming Missouri Certification scores?"

"Let's move this to my office."

Arissa's scowl tightened each time I declined his offer. As we headed in, Osbourne accepted a hot cup of coffee from my secretary with a nod. We sat down in my office and I reminded myself of my responsibility to the kids when I glanced at my doctorate in education on the wall above Osbourne's head, which I wanted to sever.

"I will not accept any offer from a drug dealer."

"Dr. Watson, as you prefer—or should I say Red?—you have built up a reputation for yourself. Why did you shoot my bodyguard?"

I did not respond to his accusations.

"He was minding his business at the gym. You didn't give Mess a chance."

I did not respond again. Distance equals one meter. I timed his reaction to me jumping across the desk with my hands going around his neck. I would reach his neck before his hands would reach mine, since he still held coffee in his right hand and wouldn't want to spill it.

"We have enough computers here. We do not need your media attention grabber. You may leave."

"Are you declining my offer, Dr. Watson? That's a mistake."

I leaned in. "Your intimidating manner does not put any fear in me. If not for Arissa being within audible range, I would have shoved my fingers through your eyeballs four minutes ago. Your last vision would be me licking my fingers while you reach for your bloody sockets."

"The blood would leave such a stain on your brown carpet. Did you realize that when you killed Az-Zhan with an ice dart?"

I said nothing.

"Yes, sir, Dr. Watson. You spend too much time on the Internet. Ice bullets? You calculated everything; except the time it takes a one-inch ice dart to melt. Your error allowed me enough time to get a snapshot." He pulled out a black-and-white photo of the wall at the Tavern nightclub and laid it on the desk. A small icicle protruded from the wall.

"I don't make mistakes. I wanted you to see what will end your pathetic life. I have one with your name engraved on it."

"The greatest of faults is to be conscious of none, Dr. Watson. Watch yourself." He took a sip of coffee and continued.

"Such a tragedy for an innocent life. Destined for fame as a music artist, and you cut that short. Shot close range right through the head. What could he have possibly done to deserve such a death, Red?"

"Az-Zhan was responsible for four brutal killings in that alley behind the Tavern. Each victim beat in the head by a blunt object. After the news headlined all of them, the murders faded. I'm sure you paid enough people to make them forget. I didn't forget, and I paid all the victims and their families back."

Osbourne leaned back as I continued.

"Before I shot Az-Zhan, I gave him a chance to live. I offered him his life if he could answer one question."

He was silent during my pause.

I smiled. "I asked him how many feet are in one mile."

"You killed my bodyguard over a fucking math question?"

"I killed him because he was a disgrace to this planet, with the potential to infect more. What kind of positive influence could he have become if he'd succeeded as a music artist? Millions of kids would sing along with a dumbass. Millions of kids would know his lyrics about making it rain in a damn strip club but wouldn't know how to calculate how many feet are in a mile. I gave him the same information when he was my student years ago. I warned him he would need math one day. And you—you should hire smarter bodyguards."

Osbourne sat back and rubbed his temple.

"Get the fuck out of my office, Osbourne."

"Young man, are you telling me where to go?"

I stood, extending my hand and pointing him out the door.

"Keep your tablets."

"I will hand you your ass on a silver platter, Dr. Watson. Expect a call from Dr. Gasen demanding to know why you overturned his approval for my donation. Have a pleasant day."

Arissa shrieked when she heard Osbourne's coffee mug shatter against the wall, five minutes after he left.

Chapter 6

Lee

Her pink Barbie helmet bobbed in between the cars parked on the street as the screaming engine of a red Dodge Charger approached. She matched her pink Black Barbie bicycle with pink streamers hanging off the handlebar grips. No brakes yet—that car ain't stopping today. Shit! I dropped my new phone as I hopped down the front steps from Grandmama's house and raced toward Juni in the street. The screen door slammed, and my ankle sprained when I cleared all the steps and zipped between a Mini Cooper and Simi's minivan. I'd worry about it later.

"You can't ride my bike, Lee."

That was the last thing she said before I dove, tackling her like a linebacker sacking the quarterback on fourth and long. I spun out of control as the front bumper of the Charger clipped my leg. Then I counted clouds in the sky in pain, thinking how Grandmama would have a fit about me knocking the screen door off the hinges. Then I remembered she died a few years ago.

I had a clear view of the underside of the bumper all the way to the back, near the front axle on my left side. Whoever owned it must not have had time to wash because bugs covered the front end. I'd tell the driver about the leaking radiator. Shit! The back of my head ached like something terrible. Goddammit! Forget my head, my arm hurt like a motherfucker. I checked my arm, covered in blood, and noticed a piece of bone sticking out of the side. Then I turned to the right and saw Simi's daughter laid across the street ten feet away with her bike on top of her. Yeah, she was crying. I must have rolled a few times because the gravel mixed with glass made their home on my tank top and hair. I smelled the rubber from the brakes. The car door opened and slammed. Simi screamed running out her front door.

"Lord Jesus! Juni!" She darted into the street.

"Mama, Lee pushed me down," Juni's ungrateful ass cried out, pinned under her bike.

"I didn't see her. I'm so sorry. I–I–I called the police." A heavyset blond woman, who looked to be in her mid-forties, ran over to Simi.

"Lady, please!" Simi said as the woman blocked her path to Juni, explaining her side of the story like she was in court already. She continued talking after Simi pushed her to the side to attend to her daughter.

"Juni, are you okay?" Simi moved the bike off Juni.

"Lee pushed me down. He's mean."

Ain't this a bitch? In my pain, I thought about how mean it is to call a six-year-old a bitch after pushing her out the way. I tried to move from under the car, thinking this woman either hopped out in a panic or was just too goddamn stupid to put it in park. My right arm spilled blood at the same rate her car leaked antifreeze. I tried to roll over and sit up on my left side when I smacked my head on the bumper of her Charger. The force knocked my head back on the pavement. Shit! After hearing the thud, Simi and the woman both looked at me as Neru joined them outside.

"God, what happened?" he asked.

"Daddy, Lee pushed me down. Beat him up."

Neru looked at his wife, then at me in a panic. He came over and knelt.

"Lee, help is on the way. Are you all right?"

"Do I look all right to you?"

A small crowd had formed outside on the neighbors' lawns. Everyone walked over to Juni and left me alone. The woman, up close in Simi's ear, tried to defend herself. What did I have to do to get some help? I got a damn bone sticking out my arm. I should have stayed in the house.

Now this woman sobbed on Simi's shoulder about how she didn't see her daughter. Neru didn't have a damn clue what to do; he's the last person I wanted to see before I died.

"Lee, what happened?"

"Your daughter was riding in the street." I stopped to cough. "I came to the door on the phone when the car raced up the street. I pushed her out the way, and now I'm laid out in this bitch. I think my arm is broke."

"Oh, you think it's broke? I got news for you," Neru said, looking at my mangled limb. "Lee, keep still, man. They should be here any minute."

"Can you help me up?"

"Better not. Your neck might be—"

"Man, my neck is fine."

I grabbed the lady's bumper and pulled myself up. Neru pitched in to help me sit with my back against the front of the car. I looked over at Juni who sat in her mom's lap on the curb, still mad at me.

"Lee, you mean," she screamed.

"Juni. No, baby. He saved your life. Mr. Lee is quite the hero." Simi then looked up at me with red swollen eyes and mouthed, "Thank you." She sniffled while speaking to her daughter about riding her bike in the street without permission. Some other people in the neighborhood came over to help me.

Someone even brought me a bottle of water. Neru stood with his hands on his hips and looked over at Simi and Juni.

"Man, Lee, I–I–I, that's my only daughter, man," he said as a tear ran down one of his cheeks. "My family is all I've got. You saved my baby girl."

"We family, bro." I replied.

He pulled on his locks while he tried to get himself together. I'd clown his ass later for crying like a bitch, but who knew what I would do if that happened to my baby girl.

"Can you call my brother for me when you get a chance?" I asked.

Why is Juni still screaming? The other noise snuck up behind me. I wished Simi would shut her daughter up. *She won't stop screaming. Why is she yelling?* I started shaking my head. Then the tears started falling down my eyes. That goddamn sound made its way to my ears, and it blared like a rock concert.

"No, no, no. Not now. I can't take this shit," I said.

"Lee, what's wrong?" Neru asked. Everyone started looking at me.

"Why is she screaming?"

"No one is screaming. What are you talking about, Lee?" Neru asked as I looked over at Juni. She appeared to be okay. Her knee had scraped from where I had shoved her, bike and all, out the way at the last minute.

Scramble

My perspective changed. Shit filled my nose. The screaming would not let up. Upside down again in my parents' car. I couldn't move. The hiss of smoke. The air bubbled from the car as it sank deeper in the ditch. The crickets and frogs sang uninterrupted as I saw my dad try in vain to reach for my mom. The steering wheel had smashed into his face, and his free arm was the only thing that could move. The shattered windshield held red freckles from his impact. The dark brown water of the ditch filled his side first.

"Dad, please."

"Dad? Lee, Lee, talk to me," Neru looked at me, confused. He couldn't understand why I kept a gun next to me while I slept at night.

My screaming mom powerless to help my dad as they sunk further down the embankment full of water. The impact had crushed her face when she thumped the windshield. The glass shimmered like diamonds in her hair. There were teeth missing when she screamed and the ones that remained were covered in blood. She looked back at me and shook her head apologizing. I noticed the rear passenger door open. I didn't see Jonas anywhere. The sound of that wheel spinning filled my ears like a beer filling a glass.

I tried standing, but Neru held me down. My mind flashed back to the scene of the accident again. Powerless, I struggled against Neru's firm grasp. I remember part of what my dad said, screaming out for his wife, Minora. The rising mud—or should I say the sinking car—muffled his voice. In a panic, he started shaking as the mud reached his nostrils. My mom unable to do a thing as she realized she's next.

"Let go of me!"

"Lee! Your arm! Relax! Relax!" Neru yelled at me, failing to restrain me with his voice. I started throwing punches at anything, not realizing I'm hitting him in the chest.

"Get off me," I said fighting him. Neru looked at Simi as she walked over. Still struggling to stand up, Neru waved her off. He danced behind me while I fought the air and wrapped his arms around me.

In the car again, the wheel kept spinning—the sound of metal on metal as the mud covered my dad completely and approached my mom. His last words were gargling and spitting muddy water like he had finished brushing his teeth. I had a free hand, unable to grab the handle of Mom's seat belt. I reached until I felt my skin rip. She remained silent.

I shook in Neru's hands, still imagining my hand fighting with that seat belt. *Shit! Faster, Lee!* I grabbed Neru's shirt behind me, but in my mind, I grabbed onto that seat, trying to free her. The bubbles popping as they came to the surface decreased until none remained as she expired.

“Sir, please, we just need an ambulance. He’s going into shock. Look at his arm,” Neru said to two approaching cops, holding their guns aimed, anticipating false evidence appearing real.

The two cops radioed to dispatch. They then told everyone crowded around to step back, pushing the bystanders away so the ambulance could have room to get into the accident scene. I heard several people shaking their heads and saying, “damn” and “that’s messed up” before I zoned out again. I couldn’t hear them talking anymore. Mucus ran down my nose and on to Neru’s arm. I cried waiting for this nightmare to end.

“Relax brother. You gotta relax. Breathe, man, breathe,” he whispered in my ear. The mud rose to my shoulders, and I called for my brother when I blacked out.

Chapter 7

Ava

I followed my boss, Hunter Bates, into his cubicle and moved a stack of papers so I could find room to sit down. I assumed he wanted to follow up with me after I'd warned him about Boland messing with his computer. He'd just gotten into a shouting match with Bonet Booker, another manager, and I thought bringing him here would cool him off. I also wanted to get started working on his recent client, South SIDY Inc. As his administrative assistant, I'm paid to cover his ass. I cross his t's and dot his i's. I'm also his den mom. I kept him straight on the hard days. The days I would buy his favorite food because he needed lunch, but he was too busy to notice. His workspace was a mess. I needed to take a day and clean this entire office for him. The glory of being Hunter's secretary.

Hunter was new to the department. They'd hired him right out of college. He had been my supervisor for a little less than a year. I had been at Wilco-Miller for five years and I knew his coworkers would have it out for him the minute he walked in here. A few older employees were trying to get promoted, as they had been here for years. Since college graduates hadn't paid their dues, certain people felt they didn't deserve to be in management right out of school. Consequently, my boss threatened them—no fault of his own.

I'd tried to warn him on his first day but he didn't listen. I understand he got a job to do but he was playing right into their hand with the after-work socializing. They did not like him. They will smile in his face and plunge a knife in his back as soon as he turned around.

The last time they set someone up, they all went out to a bar together to celebrate the new hire, Juan Evans. Well, somehow Bonet got his corporate credit card and rang up a six-hundred-dollar tab on the account. Poor Juan was unable to prove that he didn't do it, so they let him go. It's horrible what they do.

"Are you okay? You want to talk about Bonet fronting you like that?"

"Nope."

"Hunter, when you gon' clean this pig sty?" I asked with a smile, trying to cheer him up.

He looked away from me and fixed his attention on his cubicle wall. His brows hung low above his eyes and he didn't smile back, which isn't the norm for him.

"When you show up for work on time," he said.

I tried not to show his words stung me. *That's not the Hunter I work for. What's wrong with him?*

"My son got in trouble in school and I had to pick him up."

"It's not about leaving early. It's about what time you get to work. Listen, I have to document these occurrences. Yesterday was the third time this month. And today, you were late coming back from your break."

"I'm sorry, it's hard to figure out the traffic especially with all the construction on the highway." I was late this morning because I gave Dazzo a good talking-to right before I dropped him off for school. He knows that was the last trip I will make to Happy Canyon Elementary for him being disruptive in class. As far as lunch, the damn drive-thru was held up. I wanted to ask since when did it matter to him if I'm a little late from lunch. He never mentioned it before.

"Corporate policy is a verbal warning after two instances." He continued, refusing to make eye contact. This ain't the brother I laugh with talking about *The Cosby Show* back in the day before

"Pill" Cosby took over everyone's favorite dad. Hunter remained focused on the wall and went on.

"We covered that in March of this year. I emailed confirmation of that discussion. Ava, I have to write you up for being late three times. I'm sorry."

"I understand."

"No, you don't."

He clicked on a mouse and the printer behind him started making noise, preparing to print. A few seconds later the machine purred like a kitten and a single piece of paper rolled out. He grabbed it and handed it to me. I wiped my smile clean as Hunter sat back. After all I did for his ass, this was how he thanks me. Damn, those unpaid bills on my voicemail popped in my head. *I can't afford to have this on my appraisal.*

"Read this," he said and sat back with his arms folded. It was an email dated last week from Bonet to Dutch Miller, our Area Supervisor. The email was about how Hunter and Ava fraternize a little too much and he can't discipline her as necessary because they are such best friends. I hate Bonet. I wish I gave her the ass whipping she needs. She's high on the hog, and I would bring her ass back to being knee-high to a grasshopper in thirty seconds—one-minute, tops.

"These are the emails Dutch gets every day."

"That ain't your fault. You know she doesn't like you," I responded.

"The point is she wouldn't have anything to say if you weren't late." Okay, now this motherfucker was pissing me off. My chest started hurting again as my anger boiled. I counted to ten and the pains subsided.

"I'll improve my punctuality, but you know they mad at you because they are afraid of you."

"I know what I'm up against."

"You need to go smoke or something?" *All bets off—calm down, Ava.*

Boland from IT knocked on our door. He had on a red shirt. He wore a five o'clock shadow on his face and was showing signs of a receding hairline on top of his head.

"Hey Hunter, you are due for a software upgrade. I'll come back later. You look busy."

I rolled my eyes and grunted as he left.

"I've seen it too many times the five years I've been here. There's a bounty on your head. Watch it."

"What are you talking about?"

"Software upgrade, my ass. There has been a lot of traffic in and out of your cube when you are not here."

"Who?" he asked, looking up from his email.

"Take a wild guess. One you can figure out."

I squeezed my sweaty hands together.

"Boland?" He guessed as he straightened in the chair.

"Hunter, these folks here ain't no good. That's why I don't socialize with em' like you do. See, they whisper to your boss behind your back. Everyone knows Dutch—"

"Ava, we can discuss this later. I'm leaving."

He got up and stormed out his office. I walked back into my cubicle holding the email Hunter gave me. This was too much. I picked up my framed picture of Dazzo before he went to summer camp last year. He beamed at me. I lighten up seeing my baby boy smiling with no front teeth, making a muscle with his left arm.

I set the picture frame down with care as if my son was inside and started working on corrections to South SIDY General Construction. I reviewed Hunter's spreadsheets, and yep—he messed up all his entries again. The way he enters numbers, there ain't no way a company would stay in business.

My stomach gurgled as my belly told me I'd better move fast. I made my way out of the reception area. Now it's time to get before the porcelain throne. I brought my workbook, *Be the Strong One* by Joyce Joiner, and tucked it in my purse, listening for the familiar squeak of the door as I turned the handle. My shoes echoed back the steps as I caught myself in the mirror and adjusted my braids. It was too rough today to style it.

I considered shopping to make myself feel better after Hunter's betrayal, then remembered I couldn't afford it.

I meandered to the end stall and let myself in, turning the notch to lock. I used stall number four because this one had the most space. The reel turned as I ripped off sheets of toilet tissue to cover up the lid on the commode. No time for diseases, I placed two across the lengths of the rim and one across the width. My reading material leaned on the bottom of the stall door. After undoing my slacks, I took a seat.

And started crying.

Today was too much. Tears dropped from my face on to my legs and raced down into the toilet. I imagined myself in my perfect home. I retrieved my journal out my purse for days like this. I found the edge of the picture I'd ripped out of Better Homes & Gardens magazine taped inside page forty-two of my journal. Pasadena Hills Fine Homes and Townhouses. An eggshell-white two-bedroom starter home with an orange-red Spanish-style roof. A cherry blossom tree sat in my dream front yard surrounded by a matching white gated fence. Lots of spider ferns hung off the rafters on the front porch. I pictured Dazzo playing outside without worrying about speeding cars. Not worried about brothers fighting outside. He could play outside until the sun went down. I closed my leaking eyes and visualized the setting sun reflecting in the windows.

More tears fell from the weight of what I carried.

Scramble

I'd fallen in love with this place the first time I saw it driving around with Dazzo after an ice cream Sunday. Five minutes from the best school in Saint Louis. No decayed neighborhood, no Bachari, and a washer and dryer in my home. No trips on Sundays to the laundry room.

The vision of my new home began to lift off the ground. Dirt chunks dropping from the base as it slowly rose and floated away. I dug my heels in as I tried to hold on to the windowsill, but the weight was too much. I held on as long as I could, feeling the friction of life pulling my dream away from me. *I gotta hang on. Lord, I need strength.* My thoughts spiraled out of control now. *I need a raise. I can save more towards my home. I need to save my boy. This won't get away from me—I want this house.*

My vision paused as a couple of voices entered after the restroom door slammed. I reached over in front, grabbed my journal, and tucked it into my chest, leaning back on the porcelain seat near the handle. The last thing I need is someone reporting me for wasting time in the restroom.

"Are you sure you won't get caught?" It was Bonet with some woman whose voice was unfamiliar.

"Trust me. I'm nailing that bastard Hunter."

"I like Hunter. What's your beef with him?"

"Hunter ain't got a clue. You should see the look on his face every time I call him out for going to the gym instead of doing his work. He is one of these entitled kiss-ups on the fast track who thinks he's owed the world. I'm going to show him a rude awakening. He's not stepping over me for Dutch's job."

"Really? You're worried about affirmative action man? It's me you should be worried about," the other voice said to Bonet. Then I heard kissing. The sound of two lips pulling apart and touching repeatedly. Thank goodness I didn't flush yet, blowing my cover. I set my journal on the ground. I tried to see who it was through the crack in the stall but only could make out part of Bonet. While the secret couple was canoodling, I reached into my pocket, leaned up against the mildew-stricken toilet, and pulled out my Christmas gift from my only son. A secret spy pen that can hold up to thirty minutes of recorded conversation. I've been a *Get Smart* fan for the longest time. I dreamed of having a date with Agent 86, aka Maxwell Smart, after he called me on his shoe-phone. Now I'm playing spy, but this ain't no playing. A man's job is on the line. I hit the top of the pen starting the recording and raised my feet, planting them on the door of the stall.

"You should see the mess I'm cooking for Hunter. Boland agreed to log into his computer and screw up his newest account. I should have got that account, but he kisses Dutch ass so much they overlooked me. Mr. Fast-Track got a flat tire coming."

"How do you get Boland to do all the dirty work?"

"He hates Hunter too. I got him to come in at three in the morning once and access a few pornographic websites on his computer."

"How'd you get him to do that?" she asked again after a moment of more humming and the sounds of two lovers engaging each other. I shook my head in disgust and prayed that I didn't fart out my secret location.

"Men will do anything for these." I looked again and I could see the back of the woman kissing Bonet who hopped on the sink. The kissing echoed through the bathroom. The woman was standing in between Bonet's open legs while they exchanged pleasantries. I tried to get a look at the woman by looking through the crack and still, I couldn't see her face. This was almost too easy. I was grateful for my son's holiday gift, knowing that this came at the cost of four box tops from his favorite cereal, Frosted Smacks. The work of a spy is difficult.

The pain of fatigue shot down my legs. Of all the times to get leg cramps. I tried to rub them out, but they ran down the back of my legs. I held my book, stood up, and the cramps subsided. My boss better be thankful for this. Then, in my mind, I replayed our earlier conversation when he sold me up the river. Writing me up like that. I can't afford to miss a day of work and then get behind on rent. It's bad enough trying to keep the gas on and pick between that or electricity. I didn't deserve that shit.

The lovers had stopped kissing. I guessed they were freshening back up because they resumed talking. I started recording again.

"We gotta get back to work. Conference call in ten."

"Who's after Hunter? Dutch?"

"I figure if more oversights come out of his department then it will make him look bad. I'll just mess up one of our bigger clients."

"Who'd you have in mind?"

"Advanced Health."

"The big fish."

She turned on the faucet and slammed her hand into the soap dispenser.

I waited to hit the stop button, holding my breath in silence until after they left. I remained seated, staring at the pen, holding a man's job in my hands.

Chapter 8

Dr. Watson

I wiped the steam from my fogging glasses with my bloody shirt. This day was too unbelievable to comprehend. I felt the constant pouring of the hot shower flow over my face as my eyes could not hide my anguish. The steady tears blurred my vision. I brought my pulse down by calculating, with local taxes included, the dollar amount of damage incurred when I'd thrown my cell phone through the wall above the chrome faucet. The shower soaked me as I lay in the tub recollecting the day's events at work.

"He will not succeed. Education will prosper!"

I banged the side of the tile wall until it cracked, spitting a little as I erupted. No one heard my screams as the faucet dumped water on my legs, orchestrated in harmony with the smooth course of the showerhead above me. I became lost in my mind. I looked out all around my white and blue tiled bathroom but had the success of Stevie Wonder. Stanford did not appreciate my decision to step over administrative mandates and had restated the directive of successful accreditation scores, no matter the cost. Why did he joke with education? It maps a child's life. The costs of wrong turns, I dare not think. It might someday cost him his life, I reasoned. Dr. Gasen being my supervisor did not exclude fallacy. Fallacy beckons fallacy, and I would put a stop to it. He will not succeed. Education will prosper.

The cracked mirror hanging above the vanity distorted half of my face like a Picasso masterpiece while I watched a trickle of blood run down my reflection, full of memories I shared with no one. I felt the trail cross over my nose and mingle with my wet shirt, producing a pink spot. I had no time to undress after I banged my head against my vanity mirror; I just jumped in the tub. My clothes floated like buoys because of the trapped air from my sudden move to relax my troubled mind. I leaned my head back against the wall. The beautiful Grecian-Roman archway of my bathtub brought temporary relief from this confessional. I admired the architecture. Added luminosity from the window gave the illusion of expansion, in effect giving the bathroom possession of a wider landscape. The Pompeii red and deep ocean blue from the stained-glass window highlighted the elegant yet pompous archway, with the radius and perimeter accurately calculated several times. Followed by more trickles of diluted blood from the water splashing on my head, the pink stain lengthened while I replayed each of the seven times I'd rammed my head into the mirror. Having no control, the memory ran. There was no way to stop it.

Once again, I was in the Velvet Vodka Bar many years ago, surrounded by five guys ready to unleash some tension. It was closing time, and I just wanted to finish my drink before going home. After the third request to leave, I agreed, but first I had to go to the restroom. An accidental bump on the shoulder was rectifiable by reasoning, say over a beer. The owner who I bumped and bar security thought otherwise. Built like a pro-wrestler, he stood in my path, eye-to-eye. With his dark hair in a ponytail, he wore a white horizontal striped shirt and black pants. Motioning with his head, one by one, the rest of the security team surrounded the entire screen on which this memory played.

"No! No! No!"

I beat the back of my head against the hard surface behind me until I heard something crack. I debated if it was my head or the wall.

There was no time to think. I sized up five white males. Two were brothers, highlighted by the same gradual receding of their hairline. I'd say their father, standing next to them, was in his mid-sixties and highly intoxicated, which I deduced from his slurred speech. I believe it was the owner who motioned for them to escort me off the premises. I circled around to study the two pro-wrestlers behind me, who were each around five-nine, about 145 pounds and 225 pounds respectively. They were dressed like the other members of the security team in dark pants and white shirts. The two in front of me, standing next to their father, had light blue jeans and shirts tucked in to magnify their huge Confederate Flag belt buckles, reminding me of Bo and Luke Duke from The Dukes of Hazzard.

"I asked them to calm down. I did!"

I could not convince myself otherwise and turned to logic for mercy. I smacked the surface of the water, creating a violent display that ran out of the tub and onto the tile floor.

I planned to render three of them useless while I directed my energy toward the other two. There wasn't any time to measure stamina, speed, or strength.

I hurled my entire glass of Courvoisier, ice and all, at the wrinkled face of the old man, the weak link in this band of five. It shattered against his forehead, sending him over the chair behind him. No time to think anymore. I lurched in the countermotion of striking out at the old man and punched Bo Duke with a hard-left jab in his Adam's apple. I felt the diamond in my onyx-and-platinum ring crush his larynx as he grabbed his throat for air.

Scramble

Distance to Luke Duke equals 0.4 meters. While my fist was in Bo's voice box, I leaned out, kicked downward, negative fifty degrees, and thumped Luke's left kneecap to the right, snapping tendons and ligaments. His knee buckled, shifting out of place, and he let out a yelp. Luke fell over screaming at the two standing bouncers who looked back and forth confused who to help first. Four seconds passed. The old man I'd knocked over the chair had a pool of blood coming out from his hidden head. The man with the ponytail breathed heavier in astonishment at how quickly the cord of five strands was down to two. Too late to compose myself. Finish the job. Distance to a bald black man on my left front equals 2.2 meters. I ran forward, grabbed the bald black man, and twisted his neck until it snapped, then pulled my gun and shot Mr. Ponytail in the abdomen. Fifteen seconds passed. I wished for the time to counsel them on the educational benefits of non-violence as their lives deflated like the ballooned housing market.

I ran out the back door in the rain, making sure to put a bullet in Luke's forehead before departing. That would at least distract him from the pain in his leg.

That's when I had the pleasure to meet him.

The tailor.

I'd rather stab myself.

Scramble

As the rain fell against the plastic bags inside the dumpster, there were two men standing in front of me. One lit a cigar, dressed in a Giorgio Armani three-piece navy-blue power suit with a red and white striped tie. His matching fedora covered his face. The flash from the lighter revealed wrinkles of an older gentleman wearing round spectacles resting on a large crooked nose with a striking resemblance to Christopher Lloyd. He laughed, and the shriek dropped me to my knees.

The taller man next to him, who looked like he could eat the well-dressed man, stood there unaffected by the high pitch siren exiting the old man's mouth. The giant, with matted hair under a butcher's hat, was restrained by one arm of the old man as the rain soaked his white apron, already splattered with blood and yellow stains. His eyes were green and the size of half-dollars.

The gentleman halted the ogre holding a butcher knife with ease as I grabbed both my ears to muffle the whine.

"Look at him, will you?"

The older man smiled, showing teeth that looked like decrepit grave markers in a cemetery.

"Looks like you have a mess on your hands," he said.

I still had my ears covered. The old man walked over, ignoring the downpour that spotted my glasses. He grabbed my hands and lowered them from my ears one at a time. I stood when he put a hand up.

"Stay, let me have a look at you."

He examined my face and noted my scratch.

"My lord, I found him. Bruce, he has it on his head!"

The goliath, clenching his mouthful of shark teeth, grunted as he wiped the butcher knife on his soaked apron and admired his reflection in the blade.

He laughed again.

"What do you want?" I asked.

"You've been around a long time. I thought he took you away?"

"Don't believe everything you read. I need to leave."

"No, you need to stay. I can offer you my services or you can run the high risk of getting caught. You have so many fingerprints in that bar that you wouldn't make it twenty-four hours before you are sitting behind bars."

"I don't need your help."

"Oh, yes you do. Despite how much you deserve to burn in hell, I came to help you."

"What do you want?"

"I'm glad I know you already or I would consider your actions rude. Watson, always be polite and exchange pleasantries first." He smiled, then returned to the matter at hand, "Anyway, your sloppy killing in there presents a magnificent opportunity. My friend over there feeds off—let's

just say he has a peculiar preference—and you have an obsession to kill innocent people."

"They aren't innocent," I yelled.

"Your opinion is subjective. Anyway, to keep the powers that be satisfied, let's just say that I would like to clean up after you and help my friend over there put food on his table."

The scalding water from the showerhead burned the exposed skin that was partly submerged under the surface of the gathered water of the bathtub. I fought the water, splashing and kicking, but unable to escape the reality before me.

"I don't work with anyone," I said, the tailor massaging my cheek below the scar as I rejected his offer.

"It pleases me to be the first, and right now, your bargaining posture has no legs to stand on."

"Damn you."

I reached for his neck. He moved and drove his index finger into the scratch on my head. Scalding. Hot. His radiant digit became lava to the touch as the scab over the cut as old as time itself cooked. I howled, smelling my flesh burning. He laughed again, pushing his finger deeper inside my head.

"You bastard. Forget so quickly? You carry the guilt of death with you from the beginning and you will carry death on your shoulders until the end. Oh yes, I licked my lips, watching you suffer the sensation of existence on this miserable planet continue

for eons. You justify your obsession because they didn't study? If I could, I would chop you up and feed you to Bruce myself," he said laughing again, causing my ears to bleed. I couldn't take the agony anymore.

"We all have our thorns, Watson! I have that stupid idiot over there, and you have guilt fucking you up the ass. I know what you did before teaching. So many innocent people killed in the name of job satisfaction. You are so disordered it's almost like you want to get caught. See, we need each other. Help me or I will burn my finger through your dense head."

"I yield, I yield!" I grabbed my ears and bent over on my knees, kissing the ground, pleading for him to stop.

"Good. We're partners now. I'll help you now, and you can help me in the future."

The burning and screeches disappeared into the peaceful sound of raindrops as I was left alone, weeping on my knees. No sign of my tormentors anywhere. I looked at the mushy business card now left in my right hand. The tailor didn't have a first or last name. He only referred to himself as the tailor.

The showerhead faded in and out, replacing the raindrops I'd felt outside the bar alley. As I came out of my daydream in the shower, the scrape on my forehead glowed like hot metal and my ears were ringing. Government-ordered directives did not operate in the past, so I got out of the shower, dried off, and turned my attention to the present. To Dr. Gasen.

Chapter 9

Ava

"Fired foreal, Chica?"

"Girl, they canned his ass while I was out to lunch. Came back and Bonet told me she was my new supervisor. I was like, oh hell naw." I put my foot up on the wooden living room table stained with a dark cherry finish and two glass squares in the middle.

"That's messed up."

"One part of me was like, that's what his ass deserves for forgetting we need to stick together, and the other part of me was like, damn I gotta put up with Bonet."

"You still need a person to show up and break someone's jaw?"

"Girl, yeah. I would hire you to put a beatdown on Hunter too."

"What did he do to you?"

"Girl, he wrote me up for being late," I said.

"Were you late?"

"Yeah."

"So, you mad at him for doing his job?"

"He could have let me off," I said.

"*Chica, te amo, pero tengas incorrecto para eso*."

"Why you say that?"

"*¿Vencas Dazzo y tu aceptar responsabilidad*?"

"That's different, C."

"No, it ain't. You always run late somewhere. You told me you can't afford it when Dazzo messes up, how do you think your boss feels when you walk in late, and his peers assume he can't manage his crew? Same difference."

"Damn C, why are you coming so hard like that?"

"Because I'm your best friend, bitch."

"I know you are." Dazzo walked by and into the kitchen out of eyesight. I heard the faucet run and a cup fill. The plastic bounced around in the sink when he finished drinking. He waved at me on the way back to his room. I pictured my boy older, dealing with an employee like me showing up late. Another employee stabbing him in the back for a promotion. It's hard enough as it is, but I could have done a better job for Hunter. Well hell, it's too late now.

"Chica, are you going to play the tape for his boss?"

"Girl, he might fire me for recording that conversation."

"Won't Bonet do the same thing to you? You are next."

"Yeah, I figured I was next, but girl, I don't know. That dude can look at me and decide he doesn't believe a word I'm saying. What if he doesn't like me? I can't afford to lose this job, can I? I am already behind on my bills, and I promised Dazzo a new PlayStation 5 for his birthday. I can't let him down again like I did this last Christmas."

"Believe you? You recorded her? Is this the same Ava that I was talking to yesterday?"

"Girl, I gotta pay these bills."

"Ava, look, that man lost his job and you got the only clue that they set him up, and you're mad at him because he wrote you up for running late? You can't stand Bonet either and now she's your boss? Are you even thinking, Chica? I would have had that recording in his hands the day you taped it. I don't know how you sleep at night."

She asked a good question, because I tossed and turned all that night until the alarm sounded. I got Dazzo to school and pulled into the parking garage of the Wilco-Miller Accounting Firm. I heard the park brake engage when I pulled on the handle. Damn check engine light is still on. The car was running fine today, but I need to get that looked at before it gets worse.

My grandfather always said, fix a problem while it's cheap. Well, I needed to fix this problem in front of me. I was a little scared because I don't normally enjoy talking to higher-ups. I do my job and stay off the radar. For once, I got to work early. There were a few cars in the garage and I saw Dutch's BMW.

I got out and walked in. Some lights were still out. After I set my purse on my desk and grabbed my spy pen along with a few documents, I said a quick prayer. *God, if they fire me, then they fire me.* I trusted that everything would be okay. I walked to Dutch's office and knocked on the door. His secretary wasn't even there yet.

"Come on in."

"Good morning, Mr. Miller."

"Bonet, did you finish the—oh, I'm sorry. Good morning." Dutch whirled around, both eyebrows high on his forehead. I smiled.

"Good morning. Your secretary didn't arrive, or else I—"

"No worries at all. Have a seat, Ava." I sat in the leather chair and inspected his office while Mr. Miller faced me, with his left hand lifting his glasses off his nose and his right hand holding a spreadsheet. Hunter could take some notes from him on how to keep an office clean.

After a few moments, he set the paper down and looked at me.

"Mr. Miller. We need to talk."

"First off, call me Dutch. We are equals here." Yeah right, our paychecks ain't equal, but I respected his point.

"Dutch—What are *you* doing in here?"

Bonet peeked her head in the door and gave me a frown. I return her frown with a smirk.

"I called her in to review a spreadsheet," Mr. Miller waved her away.

"Okay. I'm wrapping up Prokiat AT and will have that on your desk." She left.

"She thinks she runs the place. Proceed, Ava."

"Mr. Miller, I mean Dutch, we need to talk."

"Regarding?"

"My boss."

"Bonet?"

"No, my boss, Hunter," I said.

Dutch walked over and shut the door. I fidgeted with my thumbs.

"Dutch, I know it's against the law, but I have a spy pen. I was in the restroom when I overheard Bonet admitting she set up Hunter. She had Boland add mistakes to his work. I recorded her talking about how she wanted to get Hunter fired, and then she was coming after you next."

Mr. Miller let out a deep sigh and rubbed the back of his neck as he looked at me with a frozen gaze. I felt my emotions rising—I couldn't afford to lose my job. He placed his index finger on his temple. I thought about Dazzo, and continued.

"I know I can get fired for recording someone, but wrong is wrong, Mr. Miller. You fired a kind man. Hunter and I would go over our reports multiple times before we submitted them."

"I see. Do you have the recording?"

"I do. I also have documented several instances of Boland going into Hunter's office and messing with his computer without asking." Oh god, the criminal charges if he visited kiddie porn websites on Hunter's computer. Shit can get you locked up, or even classified as a sex offender for the rest of your life.

I set the folder with the dates and times of Boland going into his office, plus the secret spy pen, on his desk. I imagined the sad look on Dazzo's face when he woke up Christmas morning and ran out to a tree with no gifts under it. I nodded at Dutch and pressed the button. When it finished playing the recording, we sat there for several minutes.

"Ava, you illegally recorded someone without their consent." *Oh shoot, here come those chest pains again.* I started breathing heavy.

"Mr. Miller, let me ex—"

"Let me finish. Even though it was wrong, you did a brave thing making your stand for what is right. I jumped to conclusions and released Hunter related to another issue, but I'm questioning the integrity of the accusations now. I can't use the evidence you have, but I have other ways to prove the recording is true. Destroy the recording. You are not to disclose this information to anyone. You did an excellent job, Ava. Thank you."

"Can you get Hunter his job back?"

"Once we get the results of the official investigation, we will make a decision."

He winked at me. I smiled and left the office beaming, not feeling this good since I first learned how to swim at age six.

After work, I overheard Boland and Bonet arguing as I walked out to the car. I leaned against the pillar supporting the three floors of the garage above me to stay out of their sight.

"If you were more attentive, you would've noticed the camera on you the whole time."

"Camera, what camera?"

"The one that got you on Hunter's computer at four in the morning."

He rubbed his head in disbelief.

"Son of a—M-my wife is gonna kill me."

"Calm down. They didn't say you were fired. Just under investigation."

"What about you?"

"I am under investigation too."

Boy, do I owe Dazzo a treat. I owe myself lunch and a half-day vacation. I didn't realize they would start moving that fast.

"Damn it, Bonet! What am I going to do?"

"I don't know."

"Well, what about you?"

He dropped his briefcase. The dull sound greeted the concrete floor of the garage as he wrapped his large fingers around Bonet's neck. She retaliated with a useless fury of punches on Boland's chest, trying to get free of his grasp.

"Let me guuuuuh."

"You lied and pinned this on me, didn't you? This was your idea! What do I tell my wife?"

His voice echoed inside the parking garage. He squeezed tight as the little hair he had slicked to the side fell down the front of his face. *He's gonna choke her to death*, I thought as he spoke, clenching his teeth and forcing out each word without moving his mouth. She was about six inches off the ground when I ran around the corner.

"Boland, stop!"

"Stay out of this."

"I'm going to call the police if you don't let go." I pulled out my phone.

He looked like a viper ready to strike. I moved closer as Bonet realized I was there. He released his chokehold and put his hands on his hips, turning away. Bonet fell on her knees, trying to catch her breath. The way it smells, I'm not sure if she would want to catch it or not.

He charged at her again. I stepped in the way of his attempted strike. He couldn't take me. I held him back as he tried to rush her again. She looked up at the two of us like a lost dog. Dog is a suitable word, but I got a better one. I faced Boland.

"Just—just go home and cool off. Don't make this any worse."

He picked up his suitcase and walked away, shaking his head. Three armed security guards approached and surrounded him. He put his hands up and looked back at us with disbelief on his face. I didn't know they had cameras in here either. I saw one guard lean into his shoulder to talk to the radio requesting officer backup. Here come the police. I looked back at Bonet and couldn't reason with myself on why I helped her and not him. She remained on the ground, holding her red neck from Boland's vice grip and coughing.

"Are you okay?" I asked obligingly, then stepped away not waiting for the answer, leaving her on her knees. I heard her whimpering. She was sniffling and rubbing her eyes. No sympathy here. I should have let him finish. If she messed with me again, then I would tell C to go ahead with that beatdown. I left after answering the security guards' questions.

Chapter 10

Dr. Watson

Life is the constant education to extract our vitality. It had been a full twenty-four hours since he insulted me with his jokes about curbing violence, yet it rattled me so much it felt like five minutes ago. I was on the daily conference call with Dr. Gasen in my office. I pushed the orange mute button on my phone and paged Arissa. Earlier today, she'd asked me about the bruises and cuts on my forehead, and I'd told her that I'd bumped into the door rushing this morning. I reassured her in my calmest tone. I stowed my plans to assassinate the director of administration under paperwork as he started our midweek teleconference call. She walked in wearing a new coffee-brown pantsuit and vanilla blouse. Her hair was back to her normal twists with maroon streaks.

"I love the new hairstyle," I said.

"Why thank you, Doctor," she replied, looking away and twirling a braid.

"Arissa, please call Isaiah Davis to the office."

"Right away." She turned to make the page when I cut her off.

"Arissa, one more thing." She turned and cut her eyes at me.

"The One-Hundred Black Men of St. Louis is holding its annual gala in a few weeks, and I was wondering if you would like to attend. Platonic, of course. It took me years to convince the local chapter I was a worthy candidate."

"Excuse me?"

"The gala. Would you like to go?"

She gave me a look as if she wanted to ask me something, but she hesitated.

"I guess it would be unusual for them to let you—"

"I'm sorry. I guess it's an awkward request, given the manager-employee relationship we have. I thought it would be a great place for you to network and interact with professional men and women. I hope you didn't feel harassed because it wasn't my intent to—"

She looked away, astonished.

"No, no, you are fine. You didn't come across that way at all. It's just that—let me check my calendar. I'll let you know."

"Superb. Keep me posted."

"Thank you for the invite, Dr. Watson."

Arissa patted down her hair with one hand to make sure she looked one hundred percent. Her cheeks blended with the streaks in her twisted hair as she walked away backward to page Isaiah.

It was time for Isaiah to learn. I am the village that will raise this child. One child at a time, I reminded myself. I pushed the mute button again.

"Dr. Gasen? I'm back on." We were also online with three other principals from elementary schools around the district.

"Clark. Just in time. We're eager to know how you're meeting the challenge of curbing violence in schools."

"Dr. Gasen, curbing violence means we have to kill violence at the roots—find the supplier of the weapons of class destruction and eliminate them. Then we must ask, where are the roots receiving their nourishment? Negative inhibitors such as unsupervised internet access, unsupervised music choices being made by children, and unsupervised access to negative role models in sports and television. Negative inhibitors must be replaced with education. We get to the root of the problem and kill it. Then we must enforce our policies of strict educational priorities and communicate that we will not tolerate any deviations. Education will kill violence."

I gave my normal pause. I hoped Dr. Gasen realized Osbourne was the root of the violence in St. Louis. Why would he stand behind him and allow him to funnel dollars into an educational facility? I wasn't buying it. I also believed Dr. Gasen himself was the other root of violence, one that I would eliminate. Solving simple math exercises on my notepad provided a needed distraction as I continued.

"We need an agenda that will lay the groundwork for a successful plan integrating enhanced security, including cameras, undercover agents as staff, and metal detectors. Leading with education, we will set the standard, and it will trickle down into the classroom."

Isaiah arrived in my office. I motioned for him to have a seat while I muted the conference call. He appeared frightened that he had been summoned to my office again. I bet he thought his mom was there too.

"Isaiah Davis. Welcome," I said after the meeting concluded. I pulled out his file and looked at his record.

"Do you have a problem with math?" He had several C-average grades in succession.

"No, sir."

"Yes, you do. C's are not acceptable. I expect better grades from you in the future."

He lowered his head.

"Isaiah, the future is now. You should ask for help with math if you're having trouble understanding. We are here to help you reach your educational goals. Look at me. I'm talking to you, man to man."

He peeked at me, then lowered his head.

"I also will not tolerate any more behavior problems from you."

"Yes, sir."

"I suggest you pick some new friends to hang around. Look at me."

I leaned back in my chair and fixed my eyes onto his.

"Your mom makes noble sacrifices for you I am sure you do not understand yet. Please give this envelope to her. Do not open it."

I handed him a white envelope, then sat back, studying my next protégé. He stood about four feet, seven inches, and was close to weighing eighty pounds—a clean-cut kid with few incidents reported. This was the first time I'd had to deal with him in the arena of discipline. I could help him.

"Would you like some lunch, say McDonald's?" His eyes lit up at the thought of not enduring another school pizza. I couldn't say that I blamed him. I half-smiled while he nodded.

"I already told your mom. Let's go then."

I told Arissa I was having lunch with Isaiah in the cafeteria and would be back in an hour. When she went back to filing paperwork, I led him outside. After checking for witnesses, I opened the passenger door of my Cadillac and let him in. I went around to the driver's side unnoticed and joined him inside.

"What do you order at McDonald's?" I put the car in reverse and twisted with one arm across the top of Isaiah's seat and the other on the wheel.

"A double cheeseburger and fries," he answered.

"I get the Quarter Pounder with cheese."

Bach's "The Well-Tempered Clavier" was pleasant background music to our discussion as I continued to drill him with answers to his math questions. I asked him about his long-term goals and shared the importance of having a career strategy before he entered college. A 1983 Caprice Classic pulled up behind me—or rather I *heard* a Caprice Classic pull up behind me. In astonishment, I placed my hand on the dashboard to gauge the intensity of the vibrating speakers from the other driver's car that drowned out my classical music. Isaiah nodded along to the rap song that shook my rearview mirror.

"You like that, Isaiah?"

He said yes and continued nodding to the beat of the Caprice's music. I suppose the driver decided I was traveling too slowly because it passed illegally on my right side. I saw Isaiah admire his candy apple red paint job. The rims were so big that the suspension hiked the car up like a monster truck. *That's ridiculous,* I thought, but he had Isaiah's attention. This must not take root.

The driver looked at Isaiah and me, then tipped his head saying what's up. I tipped my head forward to acknowledge him. Room 108, blue LA Dodgers hat, green bookbag. It just so happened he had a taste for McDonald's, too. We pulled in behind him. *I'll invite him to lunch with us,* I thought.

"Isaiah, stay here for just a moment. I want to find out where he got his rims. Maybe I can get a set for my car."

I got out and walked toward a black man in his late twenties getting out of the car. He stood about five feet, six inches, and weighed about 163 pounds. Distance equals less than one meter.

"Good afternoon, young man. My son and I were admiring your car when you passed by. What kind of rims do you have there?"

He smiled, leaning against his car door and said, "Thirty-two-inch Slick Series III."

"Slick they are."

"Man, you look familiar," he said as I stooped down to avoid eye contact. The shiny finish of the five-star dual-spoke wheels highlighted the low-profile tires. He was standing next to the driver's seat with the door open. He leaned in and turned down the radio.

"Game recognize game, right? How much do you think a set will cost me?" He turned, squinted his eyes, and tilted his head, perplexed at my statement.

"You want a set of thirty-two-inch rims?"

"Yes, I think they would look better than the banged-up factory alloys I have now. Don't you think?"

"I never heard of that before but, with wheels and tires, they set me back about ten grand," he said.

"Ten thousand dollars?" I asked.

"Yes, sir. Talk to Robbie at Rim World and he may cut you a deal."

"Okay, so what's the circumference of these rims so I'll know what to ask for when I bring my 'Lac in, as you men you say."

He laughed and said, "You will see them in the store, just point them out."

"No, no, I need to know the circumference. What's the circumference?" I stood up and got a little closer to him. They never change. He'd lost his recess when he'd neglected to wear his baseball cap properly, bill pointing forward. Yes, Room 108, row four, seat six. Distance equals 0.35 meters.

"What?"

"The circumference—the perimeter around the wheel." I twirled my finger around, giving him a hint of what I wanted.

"Man, I don't know what you're talking 'bout."

He started laughing again while I violently continued to twirl my finger. *Watson, stop it!*

"I can't remember the last time I took math, let alone figure out the circumference," he said.

"What do you mean, Darren? Come on. What's the goddamn circumference?"

"Man, you trippin'. All you gotta do is ask for them, man." I stepped closer, gripping the gun in my pocket.

"Darren Mayes, class of 1996, fifth grade at Happy Canyon Elementary, you don't know the circumference of your own rims?"

"Hold up? How the fuck you—?"

I pulled out my gun and whipped his face with the handle. He fell against his door, which was still open. I grabbed his shirt collar and pulled him so close he had a full whiff of the Sanka Brown Safari coffee I had sipped that morning. I whipped his face two more times. I clamped my arm on his bicep and the gun barrel on his abdomen. He grabbed for the side of his head where the bottom of the gun handle had landed three times and I continued.

"Listen, I'm asking the fucking questions here. You got one more try to get it right. What is the equation for the circumference of these rims? Think."

He didn't have the right to remain silent, looking at me like he had in fifth grade, so I shot him. I'm too impatient. His stomach muffled the blast but the blood from the exit wound splashed on the white interior of the car. I checked left and right for police, pushed him into the car before anyone could notice, and shot him again for being a dumbass. Thank god for silencers. I continued shooting, emptying my clip, trying to scream above my gunshots.

"I gave you the goddamn answer over fifteen years ago, and you still can't tell me. I told you math would be important later, but you were too goddamn hardheaded. Now look at you."

I tried to slam the car door twice, not realizing his leg was still hanging out. After the third try, I just left it open. I walked away in frustration then took a ten count. *Relax, Watson.* I returned to the scene to adjust him as he laid motionless in the bloody interior. After I lifted his leg and set it in the car, I sat him upright and placed his phone in his hand, making sure his cap properly fit his head. I turned the key, bringing his car to life and slowly shut the door. Isaiah's mouth hung open while I gave directions to the tailor, who said he could be there first thing in the morning. He suggested I shut the car off, then attempted again to initiate a conversation with me. I told him now wasn't a good time and ended the call quickly.

Climbing back inside my car, Isaiah was screaming, so I screamed back, "What are you crying about, Isaiah, huh?"

He leaned against the window grabbing for the handle. I child-locked the door from my side. There was no way out for him. I resumed our afternoon conversation.

"You shot him. Why?" he interrupted, scooting to the far side of the leather passenger seat next to the window. Tears were falling down his face as he struggled between whimpers to ask the question.

"I asked him a question, and he didn't know the answer. Isaiah, remember your math. You fucking understand me? In addition, that motherfucker sells crack to my people, Isaiah. A drug dealer. He had his death coming."

I beat the steering wheel with my hands as I yelled. The nerve of him telling me he can't calculate the damn circumference of his own tires. We were not reaping the benefits of our education. That was the goddamn problem with these schools. Teachers wasted their time trying to teach, but no one wanted to learn. I'm putting a stop to all of that shit. There would be more follow-ups for all my students, beginning with Isaiah.

"Is that your idea of a hero, Isaiah? Grow up. You are on notice. I'm coming for you, Isaiah. You better study your math, you understand me?"

Isaiah sobbed while I continued.

"Did you see what happened to him, Isaiah, huh?" I banged my head on the steering wheel. I heard it honk while I continued educating Isaiah.

"Answer me, goddammit."

"Yes, sir."

"Don't let me find out you called anyone else a bitch, or any other cuss word coming out of your mouth. I swear I will hunt you down. You fucking understand me?"

Isaiah sobbed, still in shock at how our conversation had changed.

"If I ever see you playing that kind of music that shakes my car, I will kick your narrow ass across the 'Show Me' state, you fucking understand me? C's in math are not acceptable. Earn another one, son. I will whip your ass to death. Do you fucking understand me?" my voice escalating.

Isaiah looked straight ahead. Tears ran down his face.

I screamed again. I let go of the steering wheel to press my hands against my head to muffle the sound from within. The high-pitched whistle reminiscent of a security alarm from a door left open shifted my focus away from Isaiah to a heart monitor.

"No, why?" I asked.

"Mr. Watson, are you okay?"

"Damn you, there is nothing you can do?"

"Do what, Mr. Watson?"

I held my wife's hand as she moaned in pain. Her blue eyes shimmered from the excess wetness that fell on her cheeks. Today, she wore the red scarf to cover her hair loss. She looked beautiful. So beautiful. I hated myself that I couldn't take away her suffering.

I am her man. I make the awful things disappear. Not this one. I had to stare her in the face helplessly as stage four ran amuck.

"Can't we try anything? Any experimental drugs?"

"Try what, Mr. Watson?" Isaiah asked as he wiped his nose.

"I'm tired of watching people die," I said.

I beat the steering wheel harder, honking the horn a few times.

"No, you're a doctor, dammit. Don't tell me there is nothing you can do! Damn you."

"I'm not a doctor, Mr. Watson," Isaiah said as the outside world and my mind collided. I couldn't tell if I was dreaming or awake.

Her soft hand lost its way in my large palm. My fingers wrapped tight as she squirmed. I glanced away, too hurt to look her in the eyes. The evening news reported details of another mass school shooting in Chicago, but the anchor's lips moved in silence, as we had muted the television hanging in the room hours ago. The pink and blue of dusk hid the sun behind the large medical building next to Happy Canyon Center for Cancer Research. A folded blanket lay in the only empty chair in the room, next to the table holding a teddy bear and the bouquet of flowers I replaced every day. She always said, "Don't bring flowers to my funeral, for what good are flowers to a dead person?" I needed to rip that teddy bear's head off.

Scramble

I didn't want to tell her the doctor had given up. I didn't want to tell her that our physician's ten-plus years of medical school only produced questions and no answers. I dropped my face into my hand and wept. She put her left hand to her mouth as seven coughs escaped. As each cough sounded off, she winced in pain. As each cough released, her wedding ring danced about her bony finger. The tape on her breathing tube loosened as she forced herself to speak.

"Henry."

Her hero stared at the floor in defeat.

"Look at me, Babe."

I lifted my face to meet hers. A single tear fell. She never called me by my first name. She always preferred my middle name, Henry. In this state, she looked unfamiliar to me. No, this isn't the woman who built many memories in our home. No, not her. She hadn't danced the waltz the evening we exchanged vows in a church on the hillside. No, she didn't cook my favorite meal six hundred and thirty-four times, not counting the one time we burned the roast because we were making love.

"I know," she said. Her normal voice replaced by a whisper. Just air escaping her throat. A tone that didn't match the woman whose finger I slid a ring onto years ago.

"It's ok," she tried to force a smile. I brought her hands to my lips. My tears fell on her wrist. I watched the tear make a trail

around to her palm and out of my sight. The second one ran along the first trail and diverged onto the floor.

"I will always love you. Cancer can't take your love from me."

The sound of the EKG monitor flatlining blended into the alarm showing the keys were still lodged into the ignition switch. I faced Isaiah Davis, Jr. leaned against the leather door. I felt the heat from my cut as I spoke with my jaws clamped together.

"Wipe those damn tears off your face before I give you something to cry about."

He continued whimpering like a hurt dog. I had plans to put him down like one if he didn't do his homework.

"Isaiah, you better study your ass off because you will not let my wife die again, you fucking understand me, or I swear I will hunt you down and empty this gun in your empty head."

We arrived back at school about ten minutes early, giving Isaiah enough time to clean up while Bach orchestrated Book Two of "The Well-Tempered Clavier." I checked my shirt for blood and buttoned my suit coat to hide Darren's red polka dots. I kept a tight clamp on his shoulder as we marched to the front entrance. Arissa was heading out as we walked in.

"Hi, Arissa. We ate outside."

"I didn't see you. How was it?" she asked.

"We took a short walk by the playground. Isaiah, wouldn't you say that was a killer lunch?"

I put my index finger to my lips as a reminder to Isaiah to keep our lunch date a secret. That made Arissa smile.

Chapter 11

Ava

"Girl, I don't know. Dazzo has been in his room studying for the past two days. He won't take a break. I had to force him to eat dinner."

"Maybe that wuppin' paid off, huh?"

"It's weird. His eyes are all bugged out, and he says he wants to understand his math. Then he asked me if I would play classical music in the house."

"I heard studying to classical music makes you smarter. Hey, Chico finally asked me out."

"Who?"

"You know, Chico at the gym. The one who can't keep his eyes off my chest, girl."

"Well?" I prompted.

"Well, what?"

"Why are you so shitty on the details, bitch?"

"Well damn, girl, gimme a second," Columbia giggled. "I was walking on the treadmill for my cool down, and I noticed he was acting strange."

"Uh-huh." I looked at the stove again. I hadn't learned last time that I'm not David Copperfield. No magic wand, abracadabra, or that Leprechaun on the box of Lucky Charms cereal would make a delicious meal appear before my eyes.

"I had my V-neck t-shirt on again, and I swear his neck will hurt in the morning because he was staring at my little sisters so much. I let him look for a minute then asked him what color my eyes were."

"Girl, stop!" I giggled, pulled some ground beef from the freezer, and threw it in the sink. I heard the frozen meat popping while the faucet ran over it. I know you ain't supposed to thaw out nothing with hot water, but I got the munchies.

"Yes, *vieja*. He turned the color of Kool-Aid Man. I thought he would run through a wall and shit." I thought of the old commercials and the many times Kool-Aid Man should get sued for destroying walls.

"Then he said he wanted to see me again. I said, 'I'll see you Friday for our session', and he said no, before that and not at the gym."

"Well good, let me know the details." I peeked in the sink where the hot water was steaming as it hit the wrapped ground beef, but it was still frozen solid. I thought maybe I could run on the treadmill while the meat was thawing, except I don't have one.

"I confronted my boss's boss," I said.

"Oh, did you, girl?"

"They both got suspended. Let me tell it. I walked out to the parking garage, and Boland was choking Bonet out. I had to step in and break them up, foreal."

"He beat me to it. You know I would have if he didn't."

"Dayuuum, C-C! Hey, hold on a second." I heard the phone beep while watching Columbia's afternoon at the gym play out in my mind. Damn, no caller ID.

"Hello?"

"Ava Minnow?"

"Speaking."

"Do you know who this is?"

"No, but you will tell me, right? No thanks, but I can save you the trouble. I do not want to refinance my car."

"We have some business to discuss."

I exhaled and clicked back over to Columbia.

"Girl, I am about to let this telemarketer have it. I'm tired of these motherfuckers calling whenever the hell they feel like it. I'll call you back."

"Okay, I'll talk to you later."

I clicked back over, upset the caller got to me. I should have let it go to voicemail.

"Hello," I exhaled. "Aren't there rules about calling at a decent hour?" It helps to put them on the defensive.

"This is Osbourne, and you have an outstanding loan balance. My records state you applied for a loan two months ago at the North County Loan Patrol for one thousand dollars. Is that correct?"

"Yeah. I'm kinda short, but I'll give you what I can."

"I want my fifteen hundred dollars back."

"Didn't you hear me say I was short? I'll pay you what I can. I can give you fifty this month." I didn't ask about his jacked-up interest rate. Twenty percent is three hundred bucks, so where the hell is he getting fifteen hundred?

"I do the negotiating around here."

"Listen, Mr. Osbourne, I can give you what I stated earlier."

"I need my two thousand tonight."

"You said fifteen hundred. Even if I had it, the banks are closed. How would I get it? I can't get that much money from an ATM."

This pissed me off. Most of the time the bill collectors would nag you, but this guy was being unreasonable. He gon' mess around and make my screwed-up credit score worse. Shit, I couldn't afford that interest rate. Why was my heart pounding through my chest? In between beats, I had a twinge of pain that shot down my sternum. I leaned on the doorway, flanked by the kitchen and living room of my apartment.

"How you will get the money is not my problem. Your ex-boyfriend Isaiah had a hard head like yourself. He didn't cooperate with me."

I heard someone banging on the door. Damn, Bachari, not now.

"Bachari, I ain't got no extra washing powder," I yelled, walking over to the door. After a few seconds, someone banged again. This dude always trying to use all my Tide. I swear I would give him a full bottle and it came back empty. I could smell him down the hall. Bachari banged again on my door, louder than last time. Damn, bro, wait a minute.

"Listen, someone is at my door. I gotta go. I'll get your money as soon as I can."

"Ava baby, I am at the door."

I stood there holding the phone.

I walked over to the curtain and dragged it. Three men dressed in black stood outside my entrance. I couldn't make out their identities because the porch light bulb was blown out. I covered my mouth in shock as they banged and kicked on the door again.

"I call the shots in St. Louis. I have a big hat and bigger cattle. As much as I would like to come in and get my money, I will not come uninvited. I left you a present. Now get it."

I let go of the curtain. I didn't make a sound.

"Ava, you are wasting my time. Go to the goddamn door and get your present."

I crept along the wall to the peephole. Looking through, I could only see the dark of our neighborhood. I heard another loud thump and the shuffling of feet. Then three car doors slammed, followed by screeching tires. Trembling, I opened the door and peeked out. I didn't see anyone but I heard a loud moaning. I looked down and dropped the phone when I saw a bloodied hand dripping onto a black sports watch. His purple bruised knuckles were scraped up like a cat took a few swipes at him. His white t-shirt covered in red specks. At first, I couldn't make out who it was because his eyes were bruised shut and his face was swollen like he got his wisdom teeth pulled.

"Daddy?"

"Back in the house—now!" I shooed Dazzo hard with my arm, retrieving the phone from the floor.

"Did you do this to Isaiah? Answer me." Isaiah's moans grew louder in my ear like the sound of an approaching truck while I held both the phone and a startled kid. I tweaked my back trying to drag my two-hundred-pound ex into the house. More pains came to my neck and down my arm. Beads of sweat rolled down my forehead.

"Now I see I have your attention, Ms. Minnow."

I felt Dazzo brush next to me.

"Dazzo, baby, please get in the house. Somebody help me!"

He started crying into my leg after seeing his superman beat to a pulp. I didn't know what to do. I yelled into the yard. Were the people who did this to Isaiah hiding in the stairwell? Dazzo remained still, just standing there behind me. I pushed him back. My back was screaming against him while I tried to drag Isaiah by the leg. The pain was too much so I stopped with him halfway inside. Osbourne spoke.

"Ms. Minnow, I'm a capitalist. I offer services. In exchange, I require the price I charge for those services. With the interest accrued on your loan, the total amount is now three thousand five hundred dollars. That would cover the services displayed on Mr. Davis for his refusal to repay his loan of one thousand dollars."

"Kiss my ass, Osbourne. Dazzo, I'm telling you for the last time to get your ass in the house—now!"

Telling him was useless because he was in front of me on his knees, lying on his daddy, crying.

"Who did this to my dad?" he shrieked.

"Baby, go to your room." I looked to my left, then my right, searching for someone who could help—or who might want to finish me off. Neighborhood Watch, my ass. These neighbors watched everything but one another around here.

"Ava? Listen to me. Shouldn't your concern be about your son's safety? He seems like a hardheaded boy. You told him three times already to go to his room."

I looked at Dazzo and saw a red light on his forehead. I was ready to wet my panties, but I had to hold it in. My heart was running sprints. I had a major migraine. The pain in my arm had traversed down my left side.

"Isaiah Jr. is as good as dead. You know that, right?"

Tears streamed down my face.

"Bang!" he yelled, and I almost dropped the phone. I can't concentrate with Dazzo crying. I was trying to figure something out. How much is in my savings? Two hundred? Checking? Shit, I just paid this month's rent.

"Bang! Bang!" he shrilled like a banshee into the phone.

"What do you want?"

"I told you what I wanted. This call should have been over ten minutes ago."

"The banks are closed. I can't get your money now." Who can I go to right now? Damn, I can't let this lunatic kill my boy. I sniffled, tasting the tears that made a path to my quivering lips.

"Oh, Ava, 'can't' shuts the mind off. Say 'how.' *How* can I get Osbourne his money?"

"Okay, okay," I said, sniffling. "How can I get your money?" I was shaking like it was five degrees outside.

"That's up to you. I want four thousand dollars in three hours. Isaiah Jr. is such a pleasant boy. We wouldn't want his life cut short."

The red light on Dazzo's forehead disappeared, and I was relieved. I glanced at Isaiah Sr. who looked like three men used him as a punching bag. I clenched my chest and leaned against the door frame, fighting away pain.

"Dazzo baby, Mama gotta make a run. Help me get your daddy in the house."

Chapter 12

Lee

“Gangsta Lee? Good morning!” Neru said, holding a cup of coffee with a smile that would make Colgate proud. “Are you too gangsta for injuries?”

I felt the full weight of the cast as it fit snug on my arm. I looked at the last person I want to see when I wake up. I should have stayed dead. Neru, the pebble in my shoe, sipped his coffee, and the smell of his cat-urine breath only validated my survival of the accident. I groaned in pain, grabbing for the back of my head only to touch the surgical wrap. My other arm was in a white cast and light blue sling. My memory was fuzzy and I felt groggy as I came to. I wiggled my toes under the covers in the bed and saw my neighbor sitting in the chair next to the IV that was running into my free arm. I raised the bed to see the TV, head hurting like no tomorrow. I had a headache THIS BIG, and Excedrin ain't gon' do shit for it.

Neru grinned like he's been awake since the rooster crowed.

"Gangsta Lee, the neighborhood hero. Can I get an autograph, or are you too gangsta for autographs?"

"Man, shut up," I snapped.

"I didn't know gangstas cry. 'I'm a man. Shit. I'm a man. I handle mine,'" he said that last part mimicking my voice. I tried reaching under the pillow for my nine-millimeter and had no luck.

"How are you feeling?" His tone became more serious.

"Not bad for getting the shit knocked out of me. Where's Jonas? Is he here?"

"Down in the cafeteria. We've been here for about six hours."

"What time is it?"

"Damn, gangsta! No watch? I thought, gangstas—"

I cut him off.

"C'mon, man. Stop bullshitting."

"You've been asleep all day. It's about ten till seven, Darvin."

"Who?"

"Gangsta Lee with a nerdy middle name," he laughed. Some people have the gift of entertaining themselves.

"Do all gangstas got dorky names like that?"

"Who told you my middle name?" I asked.

"Well, I called your brother like you asked before you passed out, and he met us as soon as we arrived here in the ambulance. I overheard him telling the receptionist when he gave her your admitting information."

"You rode with me?"

"I know that's not gang—"

I cut him off again. "Thanks, man. I appreciate you riding with me."

"Hey, it's the least I could do after you—"

He paused, and his eyes welled up again while he looked away. Someone knocked on the door. After Neru said "it's open," Juni darted around the corner followed by her brother Kenji, holding Simi's hand. She ran over and leaned against the bed by my leg, next to her dad. It was so high I could only see her head. Simi put her arm around Neru, who was wiping his eyes, and looked over, smiling.

"Hi, Darvin," Juni said.

"Don't ever call me that name again."

"Okay, Darvin."

I shook my head and looked back at Neru, getting emotional.

"Hey. You all right?" I asked her, knowing I didn't give a shit. Okay, maybe I gave a little shit about that little shit.

"I'm okay. Look! I got Snoopy Band-Aids on my knee and elbow." She lifted her leg, trying to show me her Band-Aid with the dog lying on top of his red house.

"I made you something. Look!"

She reached in her mom's purse and unfolded a picture of me with a gigantic head and droopy pants. I'm sure the pants were her dad's idea. She had me flexing my muscles and a big grin on my face, all made with one thick-ass blue crayon.

"You are all she's talking about, Lee. You have a little girlfriend now," Simi said.

"Don't hospitals have rules about visiting hours for kids?" I asked, looking at an invisible watch. Simi slapped my arm and smiled.

I ain't forget about her pointing and screaming at me. I smiled at Juni, giving her the impression that I liked the picture, but inside I laughed about that thick ass blue crayon. *Damn Juni, you got seven other colors to choose from. What the hell?* What if Simi knew my opinion on her daughter's ugly artwork? I scolded myself for making fun of her picture when Jonas walked in, hugged the kids, and nodded to Simi.

"What's up, Superman?" he asked me while he gave Neru a handshake and a hug.

Shit was clear as glass now. I watched Neru pick up and hold his girl. I pictured Mom picking me up. I wanted that.

Gone now. Jonas walked around to the other side of the bed and pulled up a chair. I was reminded again of the spinning wheel draped over my head like a halo as the chair legs scraped the tiled floor of St. Matthew-Mercy Hospital.

"So, you are the neighborhood superhero?" Jonas asked.

I didn't answer him again. Neru laughed, and Simi love-tapped his chest. I glared at Jo like he needed to shut the fuck up fast.

"Jonas, we need to talk."

Simi and Neru looked at each other, then at Jonas, who shrugged.

"It's getting late. The kids have school and all." Simi broke the silence.

Neru stepped forward, shook my hand, and said he'd be there the next day and every day until we were back on his porch talking trash again.

Jonas sat back and rubbed his head when the door shut, leaving the two of us alone.

"I need your help to get Rogan."

"What?"

"Rogan Stone. Do I have to spell it out for you?"

He just sat there rubbing his head.

"Jonas, we both know he deserves what's coming," I said.

"Lee, this is stupid. You had a rough day. Let's not get into this now."

"You're not going to help?"

"Lee, I got a job. A house. Do I have to explain to you how dumb this is? The scary part is that you are serious," he said.

I squeezed my fist tight. My mom smiled at me in the car. I keep my teeth clenched when I'm pissed. I didn't give Jonas time to react as I shot out of the bed and gripped his shirt with my bare hands, ready to lift him by his collar. I knocked over the IV and a heart monitor not connected to me, which started beeping out of control when I reached for his neck and pushed him against the wall. I heard the food tray roll to the side and my dinner fall to the ground in between my breaths. My broke arm was throbbing in its cast.

"This is serious. I'm doing this for mom and dad. Look at Neru's kids. We deserved that and he took that away from us, man. Then, he's given a hero's welcome and you act like nothing happened?"

We struggled back and forth as he gripped my arms and tried turning me to gain advantage. We'd fought many times and he won most of the contests. He gained control and pushed me against the wall.

"Calm your ass down, or I will do it for you. One broke arm is enough for the day, don't you think?" he asked.

He was lucky I was banged up and not up to par. I relaxed, and he sensed a forfeit, letting go of me.

"Lee. If you think killing Rogan Stone is what mom, dad, or your grandmama would want, then you need some medication."

I yielded and turned my back as the nurse walked in. For a minute, Jonas and I stood in the quietness and admired how quick we made a mess out of the hospital room. Leave it to me and my brother to destroy some shit. The nurse rolled her eyes, turned, and walked back out. Jonas followed, bumping my shoulder as he passed.

"Have it your way, bro," I said.

"You are out of your damn mind," he replied walking away. I was the only one left to listen to my rage in the empty room. My mom's crimson smile haunted me again. I knocked over the chair and leaned against the wall to get my breath. Reaching for my cell phone, I dialed up my boy Hardhead, ready to handle my shit.

"Hello."

"Sup, dirty? This Lee."

"What are you doing?"

"I'm at the hospital. Come get ya boy. I'm ready for a ride." I kicked the IV bag and stand that my brother and I knocked over during our struggle.

"I got you."

"Let's go see Della. I got a taste for some eggs," I said.

Chapter 13

Dr. Watson

I washed my hands to prepare for dinner. I only hoped that Dazzo had understood what I'd done was for his own good. I hadn't meant to yell at him in the car, but I wasn't getting through to him about the priority of a good elementary school education. He might be confused now, but he would see the good of it later in life. I pulled out a saucepan and a measuring cup for pasta Alfredo, my favorite. My hands shook as I thought back to Dr. Gasen and his poor choice to accept Osbourne's gift of those tablets tainted with money from the sale of drugs to our people. He was a worse fit than Osbourne for public office. They must work as partners. Yes, Osbourne had worked his way into Stanford's pockets. I will bury them together. There, they could plan their corrupt schemes where they belonged—in the cemetery under the daisies adorning their grave markers.

I grabbed the butter and milk from the refrigerator and added the required measurements. I sliced one pat of butter and set it on the micro-scale. 8.75 grams. Forty-eight pats of butter equal one pound, so one pat equal nine grams. I sliced another pat into thirds then added the full pat and the slice to get the exact amount of eleven calories to the boiler. I poured one-fourth cup of milk into the measuring cup. Damn it! I couldn't tell if the one-fourth was measured at the line, or below the line. I poured out little increments until the rim of the top of the milk touched half of the thick red measuring marker. Whew! A tedious but worthy task. Yesterday I measured all the egg noodles to eight inches before they boiled for thirteen minutes and seventeen seconds, then let them rest for twenty-two hours, six minutes for the perfect texture and consistency. I set the stovetop to four hundred and nineteen degrees measured with a thermal imaging probe thermometer, watching for the pot to boil, despite my mother's stern warning against such actions. That was the only thing she was stern about. Her life thrived on chaos. Walking and chewing gum, a front-page newsworthy event in her mind. The only thing she could focus on was nothing, and even that lasted only a few seconds.

Three minutes passed as the bubbles filled the base of the pot while the temperature escalated. My anger rose again. Osbourne will fail. I had to plan his execution. I must not fail. The community depended on it. We must thrive. I am the one who will eliminate Osbourne and prevent him from succeeding in office. Education will stomp out ignorance.

"Education will stomp out ignorance!"

I threw the pan of boiling water to the floor and watched it circle a few times, then stop. Damn it! A few drops splashed on my face and glasses. I felt the hot water singe my skin. I didn't mean to splash Dr. Gasen, who was sitting on the floor with his back against the wall.

"Dr. Gasen, don't you agree that education will stomp out ignorance?"

He didn't answer. The boiling water soaked into his navy-blue blazer, white shirt, and dark khaki pants. The hot water also matted down his hair and dangled it right above his eyes. His posture was horrible. He should know that resting in that position will cause long-term back problems. I stomped him with the heel of my shoe, landing on his sternum. The force of the blow caused him to slide lower. I thought about cleaning the bloodstain that originated where I shot him in the head and trailed behind him when he slid down the wall. The exit wound left a mess I'd rather clean myself than explain to the housekeeper. It also made a mess of his light blue silk tie. Blood is hard to wash out of silk.

Scramble

Dr. Gasen's last words were quite encouraging after I'd told him about my afternoon with Isaiah. He liked the part where my former student's leg shattered after I slammed his car door on it three times for not understanding basic geometry. He called me a sick bastard who had no place interacting with children. I responded by telling him I was the best thing that could happen to a child. I am the savior that will enlighten this community and I will take the high road to do it. I banged my forehead against the wall until the plaster broke through where Stanford's blood trail originated. I had tried my best to reason with him as I unpacked my grocery bag earlier in the evening. Our argument escalated when he refused to see my point of view on the hypocrisy of Osbourne's donation.

"Dr. Gasen, it is preposterous that we accept those tablets. Do you know the sources that funded the purchase?"

"Clark, who cares? It's a donation and we need all the help we can get."

"Damn it, Stanford, he's grandstanding, and you know it!" I slammed the third onion on the table preceded by two glass containers of oregano and parsley, now shattered because of my rising temper.

"Clark, the decision is final. We keep the tablets. This shithole of an elementary school is not getting the public funding we need. We need to overlook the morality of things until the situation improves."

Scramble

A shithole? I had a drug dealer to take down and was not in the mood for his droll remarks about the decline of the schools, so I unloaded my frustrations with my gun. He gave Osbourne an inch, and it would cost everyone a mile. Osbourne's display of charity will only add fuel to his run for public office. I didn't know if Stanford heard my logic and reasoning over the three gunshots I fired after he overruled my declination of Osbourne the tablets. Maybe I was angry he censured my afternoon teaching moment with Isaiah. I scolded myself for missing him the first two times. My aim is better than that.

I picked up the pan off the ground and slammed it against the countertop, chipping the granite finish. Eating here was useless. Dr. Gasen's bloody body and his negative attitude had spoiled my appetite for pasta Alfredo. I was still hungry, though, and scrambled eggs would hit the spot. *Della will take my mind off things*, I thought. I grabbed my coat and walked to the Waffle Diner, brainstorming ideas on how to dispose of Stanford's lifeless body.

Chapter 14

Ava

I only made it down the street for ten minutes. I'd left after I convinced Dazzo to be a big boy and watch his daddy. I shook so bad I had to pull over at the gas station. From the rundown parking lot, I called my mom.

"Mama, listen to me; I can't explain it now, but I need to know if you still have Daddy's shoebox with the rainy-day money."

"Let me check." I heard her set the phone down.

I miss my daddy. Warren Minnow passed away when I was a kid. He promised we would use the allowance I put away in our secret place to buy a puzzle on a rainy day. Well, I kept saving one dollar from my five-dollar weekly allowance, and Daddy always matched it with a dollar. He never let me touch it, but he promised we would when the day was right. Often, I imagined the day he would look out the window and say, "This is it." We would sit down while a storm lashed the windows and piece together a puzzle of a girl in a wheat field. That day never came. I had thought puzzles must be damn expensive because we never seemed to have enough to get one. I never comprehended he was teaching me to save money. I thought I would be dead by the time I could sit across from my dad and put a puzzle together. Now I was sitting in my car wondering how to get out of this unbelievable situation. I could hear my mom approaching the phone.

"Ava honey, I didn't see it." A car playing loud music pulled up next to me to use the air pump. I heard the door slam after a teenager got out, then the yanking of the hose.

"Did you check all the vents?" I asked.

"If you need money, baby, I can go to the bank first thing in the morning."

My mind wandered back to the assassin's red light centered on my Dazzo's forehead. I gripped the steering wheel, wet from my sweaty hands, and thought about the worst that could happen if I didn't get the money. I saw an image of Dazzo lying motionless in my lap, blood all over me. Why did I leave Dazzo there with Isaiah? Dispatch said the paramedics were on the way to pick up Isaiah Sr., but I was certain he would refuse to go because he didn't have insurance. He had to have broken bones somewhere on him. Maybe a concussion. He'd been conscious when I left, with apology after apology in between deep breaths of pain. This time it wasn't all his fault. Besides, Dazzo could call the police if someone tried to break in. But would they help?

"Mom, I need you to go to my house to make sure Dazzo and Isaiah are okay."

"I thought—Did he hit you?"

"I can't talk now." I was running out of time and she still wanted to ask questions. I pulled out the gas station and headed north. Shit. I'd kill Osbourne if he harmed my baby. Why did I leave him there?

"Baby, whatever it is you're going through, let's pray about it now."

"Mom, I don't have time to pray."

"That's exactly when prayer is needed."

"Mom, call me when you get to my house."

Lord, if I took the time to pray, I'd have been dead. I needed Columbia, so I called her.

"Hey, girl, you got a second?" I didn't allow her to answer. I started crying like I fell out my chair when I was six years old. My daddy wasn't there to pick me up.

"He's talking about killing my baby, Columbia. I won't let him do it. Dazzo's all I've got."

"Isaiah! Betta not be. My brother's ready to wup that ass. Hold on let me—" For Isaiah's sake I cut her off.

"No, no, not him. Osbourne."

I had one hand on my heart. It felt like a panicked bird fluttering around in a birdcage.

"Slow down and tell me what's going on," C said.

"I took out a loan from Osbourne to cover some bills, and now he wants it all tonight—in two hours. Isaiah took a loan from him too. Osbourne beat him up and left him at the door. He looks like he got ran over by a truck. Osbourne told me I have to pay for both of us."

"Let me run to the ATM."

"C, you can't get four thousand dollars out at once."

"He trying to punk you, girl. I gotta gun for him. He beat up Isaiah for real?"

I didn't tell her about the red dot on Dazzo's forehead. Something triggered in my brain. I reached under the seat with my free hand and pulled out a leather bag. I veered into oncoming traffic, clutching my heart as cars beeped at me. *Calm down. Calm down. Get back over.* The pain in my arm shot up to my neck.

I unzipped the case and pulled out a .38 revolver. Confidence surged with a piece in my hand. The finish was all black and the shiny weapon fit snug in my hand.

Scramble

The chrome accents of the bullet chambers and barrel reflected the neon sign of the Waffle Diner as I drove in and parked the car. I knew the money at Mama's house was tucked away in a vent. It was not enough, but it would buy Dazzo another day. I didn't have time to drive a half hour to get it. *Borrow it, then pay it right back.*

I looked across the parking lot at the diner. Della had told me on her busiest days they could ring up four thousand dollars. The smell of hot sizzling bacon filled my nose and my mind with nostalgia of waking up on Saturday mornings and watching cartoons with my daddy; first the Smurfs and then my favorite, Road Runner and Wile E. Coyote. The register doesn't get counted until twelve fifteen. I missed my daddy. I needed a plan.

"Girl, we're in this together. Where are you?"

I forgot why I'd called her. I didn't tell her what I was planning to do. I was too busy eating cereal, waiting for Bugs Bunny to come on TV. And now the pain was gone too.

Chapter 15

Dr. Watson

"Clark, you need to get more rest, honey."

"I know, Della. It has been a rough couple of weeks."

"Teachers work too hard for little money. You need a vacation. I'll go place your order. Two and one-fourth eggs scrambled at two-hundred and seventy-five degrees for four minutes and fifty-two seconds, one ounce of shredded Monterrey cheese, and two ounces of onions. Tilt the plate and let the runny part drain for three seconds."

I nodded, amazed at her memory. The remnants from my last sip of coffee trickled down the ivory mug. I concealed the notebook containing bullet items to assassinate Osbourne as Della refilled my cup. Her words contained so many hard truths, yet it was always a pleasure to hear them. A wiry five-foot-three redhead in her mid-seventies who said exactly what was on her mind.

I first met her here over twenty years ago after a long day at work. While waiting to be seated, I noticed she had a special bond with her customers. She stared at me when I gave her the order with my terms for preparing my meal. She didn't look confused reciting from memory my order back to confirm the accuracy. Impressive. She was the first waitress ever to get my order correct down to the drain time for the eggs. We made small talk while I ate, and she passed by tending to other customers. When I finished, I found myself on the receiving end of a math quandary. She sat down with me to take a break while I enjoyed coffee after my meal.

"Della, that's impossible."

"Why would I lie to you, honey? You can look at any sunflower and the spiral pattern of seeds in the bloom will follow the Fibonacci sequence. Mother Nature is a mathematician."

Impressive.

I came back in the following Monday and stood at the register. She noticed me after I stood still for three minutes.

"Della, last Saturday I drove approximately one hundred and fifty miles into the country. I found a field three miles off the major artery of Rolla, Missouri. I sampled twelve random sunflowers in the middle to make sure it was a pure selection. To confirm, I drove

another fifty miles and drew a random sample from another field, and yes, you are correct."

She looked at me with her celery green eyes and smiled. "Honey, why didn't you just go to the florist down the street?"

Impressive.

We've been friends ever since.

One of Della's lessons was that when tragedy strikes, people will say that time heals; that time was the master healer of all wounds. She challenged that notion because she believed there was no healing. Healing was an illusion—the scar never disappears. No one heals from a wound; we learn to deal with it. Time was a dealer, not a healer. No one can get over the loss of life. Over time, we can only accept it as a part of us. She referenced her sound argument from the shootings at Columbine High School, Virginia Tech University, the movie theater in Colorado, and Sandy Hook. The families of those victims still shed tears, yet they work, they play, and continue to eat their eggs. How unfortunate that unity requires a blood sacrifice. Americans had the resolve to put aside our differences and move forward. Only in the ripped and mangled shrouds of death do we come together as a country.

I always wondered what she did prior to working here. I never asked because we always ended up having a dialogue that changed us like two chemicals reacting for the better. Della's heart beats in harmony with the Waffle Diner. She once told me she convinced the original owner to repaint the diner yellow so cheerfulness surrounded patrons while they enjoyed their meals. Her claim-to-fame adage was: if the order wasn't right, it's because the customer made the mistake. I've been coming here for the past twenty years and she hasn't messed up my order once.

She was right. I needed a break. The ongoing school problems and Stanford's lack of empathy had worked my nerves to the point of exhaustion. I must carry on because the next generation needs a good educational foundation. I feel panic-stricken, wondering what consequences lie in store for them because of the poor choices made by this generation. Our children inherited the poison of greed that has authority in this world. Education is the elixir to heal the child afflicted by these cancers. I was taking another sip of fresh coffee when Della's words of wisdom came true. Time reopened a nasty wound.

Osbourne entered through the doors of the Waffle Diner. Bearing a striking resemblance to a former St. Louis Cardinal baseball player and Morgan Freeman, he was well-dressed in a charcoal gray pinstripe suit, eggshell white shirt, and navy blue tie. How fitting. A suit for his last meal, not that he knew it was. I reunited with my gun in my trench coat, brushing the shaft with my index finger. *Nothing will stop me from killing him now.*

Momentary paralysis hit when his new bodyguard walked in behind him. Victor Goodson, enveloped in a black leather coat, black jeans, and a white t-shirt under a silver chain, made his way over to Osbourne's booth and sat with his back to me. Not surprised. I can't settle for a field goal. This play needs to put seven on the board.

"Good evening, Della," he said.

"Osbourne, how are you doing?"

"Please call me Mr. Osbourne. I'd like a cup of coffee."

I shot Della a glance, and she fired back a look of genuine disgust, then continued.

"A cup of coffee for you, too, Victor?"

"Yes, Della, that will be great," Victor replied, turning to look back at me with no change in expression.

Maybe he's undercover to get close enough to kill him. But I doubt it. Just like the rest of this corrupt city, I'd bet the farm and the chickens that Mr. Goodson has fallen victim to the almighty dollar. His poor decision will cost him his life tonight.

I sipped my steaming cup of coffee, observing Della reluctantly filling theirs. Her hand rattled the tilted carafe and coffee spilled over the edge of the rim.

"Oh god, I'm sorry," she said and took a towel to wipe the table.

Distance equals seven meters.

"Della, that's not like you. Are you okay?" Osbourne asked her as she tucked the towel in her back under the belt securing her uniform.

"Long night. I'll be right back to take your orders."

"We are ready now," Osbourne stated.

Della took their orders while I continued an assassin's inspection.

"I'd like two eggs sunny-side up. Sausage, bacon, and a side of grits."

"And for you, Victor?"

"Please call him Mr. Goodson, Della. I thought we had this discussion," Osbourne said, staring at me. Della looked up and sighed.

"Mr. Goodson, how can I help you?"

I'm sure Della wished she'd spilled that coffee in his lap. I'd like to tell her not to worry because this will be the last night he harasses anyone.

There are too many people here. Too many innocent bystanders. My killer instinct disagreed with my argument. There was no time like the present. My targets laughed and appeared to be in good spirits while I searched for a clean shot. A row of stools preceded three booths, all filled with customers. The shot would have to graze their necks and penetrate Victor's back to hit the target. Datum: Calculated exit velocity of bullet penetrating through

Victor's chest, four meters per second. Datum: Target velocity required to penetrate one Armani shirt with forty percent cotton, sixty percent polyester blend, twenty-five meters per second.

As Della was walking by with another table's order, Osbourne stopped her.

"Della, please let Dr. Watson know that his meal is on me tonight," he said.

Damn it! I clenched my fist around my pencil and shook as Osbourne winked at me. Victor turned around to look again and offered no change in expression. I rechecked the calculations in my head three times with no success. This must not prosper! My clenched hand speared my other hand on the table with the pencil. I winced, realizing the magnitude of my actions after I snapped the pencil in half.

"Holy shit! Sir, are you okay?" a bald black man in his late thirties sitting in the neighboring booth asked. I did not return an answer or a look.

"Look at him. He's bleeding all over the table."

I grabbed some napkins and wiped my mess. I continued my survey of the diner, my gaze uninhibited by the commotion I'd created with half of a pencil pierced through my shooting hand. I got up and walked toward the bathroom. Della ran toward me.

"Clark, what's wrong today? Let me take a look."

"Della, I'm fine. If you could just wipe off the table for me, I'd be grateful. I cut my hand by accident and I left a few drops of blood."

"George Washington once said worry is the interest paid by those who borrow trouble. Get yourself together," she half-smiled and went back to clean my table of the smeared blood.

I headed toward the bathroom, passing Osbourne and Victor's booth. I nearly knocked the door off the hinges to the restroom. A groan echoed through the room as I extracted the broken pencil from my hand.

Chapter 16

Lee

"Man, you did what?" I demanded.

"Am I stuttering, Lee?"

As we were rolling down the street in Hardhead's new car, he told us how he had borrowed it from this old woman.

"Man, these Buicks are nice. The suspension is firm and it has heated leather seats. Power locks and tilt wheel."

"Are you trying to sell it?" I asked, remembering the time of year. I turned off the heated seats.

Ghetti passed me the bottle of Hennessy.

"Anyway, I was standing in the middle lane of the intersection ringing my bell and asking people to fill the boot for charity."

"Wait a minute," Spaghetti chimed in. "The firemen raise donations with their boot, and the Salvation Army has the bell and the kettle. You got the shit mixed up."

"It's called taking it to the next level. Quit interrupting the story," he said.

I took a swig of the elixir and passed it back.

"Yeah, dog, no lie. They ask us for donations all the time, so I thought why not? It's right on time for the holidays," he continued sagely.

Ghetti offered him the bottle, but he declined. I'm glad. Man, he couldn't drive a lick sober, as he continued to weave in and out of traffic. I hated riding with him under the influence.

"You are worse than Wal-Mart, moving Christmas season up every year," Spaghetti said.

"Man, I got the car. You need to appreciate that. Nobody got hurt and we got a clean ride for the evening. Well, to continue my story before you two rudely interrupted. The old lady drives up and rolls down her window, telling me how bad it is out here and how she hopes things will get better after she drops a quarter in the boot. I looked at the quarter inside the boot, and I got pissed off. That makes things better? I asked her what her plans were for the day, and she said was meeting a girlfriend to go shopping."

"Man, c'mon. You making this shit up?" I asked, laughing.

"Shut up, Lee. Anyway, I looked down at the quarter, pulled my gun out, and said, 'Today your car is your donation. Now step out of the car, please.'"

"Man, everyone got a description of you," I said.

"With a Santa Claus cap on? So what? We dump it in a few hours anyway, right?"

"Well, let's do this quick. Spaghetti, make sure this dumbass dumps it after you drop me off."

"Drop you off? Hey, I'm hungry too. Lee, man, are you sure about this?" he replied.

"What?" I asked.

"You just released yourself from the hospital. Man, it's been a long day."

"You sound like my brother. Did you talk to him too?"

"This ain't a good idea. I ain't feeling it anymore."

"Hardhead, stop the car."

"What?"

"Stop the car and let this bitch out."

"Lee, look, I'm just telling you not to throw your life away over this bullshit." Ghetti leaned back on the tan leather seats. He picked up a magazine lying next to him, rolled it up, and beat his leg with it. I looked back into his eyes.

"You think my parents dying is just some bullshit?" I noticed that Hardhead kept driving but had his head turned away like he didn't want any part of the discussion.

"I didn't mean it like—"

"You said it right. It is bullshit, and it's bullshit I should have dealt with. I'll tell you the fuck what. Let's trade shoes, bro. Let's watch your mom and dad sink in a ditch and you can show me how to handle it. You weren't in that car, so you ain't got a damn clue. You watch your mom helpless as she drowns in shit-water, then come tell me how I need to deal with it. Until that happen, shut ya ass up."

"Lee, listen. That was some tragic shit, but you gotta move on. This ain't you. Revenge won't solve anything. This won't honor their memory. You gon' still feel bad after you kill him. Acknowledge the sadness of your parents' death as long as that takes and learn to let it go."

"I still have dreams about that night!"

I beat the closed door of the glove compartment, sat back, and shut my eyes. That motherfucker had got away with murder. Case closed. Just like his casket gon' be when I'm through with his ass.

"Ghetti, I am doing this with or without you. This is me moving on—like you said." I looked out the window at the homes and streets we passed in north St. Louis. "You can bail if you want to."

He pointed at Hardhead in response to me. "You ever jumped out of a Buick doing fifty in a twenty-five?"

Hardhead came out of his silence as we pulled into the diner. "I swear you two sound like my two girlfriends fighting over me. We are here. Let's eat."

Whoa! That Henny kicked in. The more I kept drinking, the funnier Head's jokes became. After I stepped out, I took a final swig to calm my nerves, tossing the bottle between our car and a black Cadillac parked next to us. I heard it roll under the car as I pushed the door open with my broken arm. They packed the diner tonight, with the sounds of metal forks chipping on the ceramic plates and constant chatter from patrons eating and talking. Man, I couldn't wait for Della's eggs—scrambled omelet with Mexican rice, chorizo, beans, and con-queso. She named it The Le'Angelo after me. I scanned the room, wondering if she worked tonight. Yep, I found her in the corner. She winked at me while cashing out a patron as we walked in.

"Hi, honey! I like those cornrows, sexy." Hardhead elbowed me and whispered something about a sabretooth which I ignored.

"Hi Della, you know what I want, young lady?" I asked, smiling. Della brought me into the moment and took my mind off other things.

“Of course I do, sweetie. But I will double your order to put some meat on them bones. Does anyone feed you?”

“You know I like to eat, mama,” I said.

“I can’t tell. You are way too skinny for your height.”

“Chicks love a slim man,” I countered.

“The only things that shouldn’t be slim on a man is his wallet and his—” she said, stopping mid-sentence with a wink.

Hardhead and Spaghetti couldn't hold back their laughter.

“Why is Howard laughing? Because a sabretooth said it?” Della asked, arms folded with a smirk.

“Whoa, how did she know I said that?” Hardhead whispered in my ear. Della smiled.

“Damn, I’ve been called a cougar, but a sabretooth? I’m offended.”

“Stop it,” I quipped, looking over her shoulder. “Is that—” Osbourne’s suit shined in the reflection from the window. Sitting with his back to me about eight booths away, he sipped coffee with another man. I hadn’t seen him since our last encounter. I think I should keep it that way.

“Yes, child. He just walked in. I’m trying to hurry and get him out of here.”

“Well, we gon’ sit over here.”

I wanted nothing to do with him. My mind remained on my target, who I’d noticed smoking out back when we got out of the car. Della grabbed my hand before I sat in the booth next to the door.

“Lee, is something wrong?”

“What are you talking about, Della? I'm good. Howard, Ghetti, tell her what y’all want.”

“Baby, I already know. Bachari wants a steak and cheese omelet with onions, and Howard wants three eggs over easy with two links. Side of oatmeal.”

“Damn, Della, do you forget anything?” I asked, impressed with her memory.

“Only the past. I suggest you do the same. I can feel the weight you are carrying, sugar.”

She squeezed my hand and rushed off.

Chapter 17

Dr. Watson

I read the graffiti on the walls of the diner bathroom to distract myself from the encroaching pain. Licking the sweat that rolled down my face, I lifted the broken pencil from my tensed hand. The greenish veins, emptied streams of blood, running toward my wrinkled fingers. A dime-sized red circle quickly formed around the wound where the Faber Castell Number 2 once stood like a dead tree that lost its flourished branches. Red droplets stuck to the rim of the basin. The door open and I glimpsed Victor going into an empty stall to relieve himself. Moments later, his urine plummeted into the pool at the base of the urinal.

"Long time no see, Red."

"Mr. Goodson, a pleasure to see you. Don't call me by that name anymore."

"Okay, Doc. Are you here for Della's special too?"

"The usual," I said.

"I remember those late nights after our assignments and we'd come in and order the special. Scrambled eggs with ham, pineapple, and shredded cheese. I always had a taste for the special."

"I never had a complaint." I heard Vegas zip up and flush. I dried my hands at the paper towel dispenser. Vegas walked over to the sink I was using and pushed the button for the soap.

"You left the water on for me? Thanks."

"Why are you here with Osbourne?"

"I have my reasons, and they aren't any of your business," he said while I dried my hands. My hand was still bleeding, so I wrapped more towels around it.

"You sold me out for him?" I asked, tossing my paper towels with the broken pencil in the trash. "Your treachery is unacceptable."

"Motherfucker, if you think I still hold one inch of alliance to you or the government-ordered directive then you are sadly mistaken. Let's just say they are behind on paying me for some completed jobs. One of them being the job to kill the man I now work for."

"Vegas, I gave my life to this agency. How could you betray us?"

"They betrayed me when they didn't send the direct deposit for killing him."

"You didn't finish the job. Osbourne is eating waffles right out there." I pointed to the dining room.

He balled up his paper towels, shot them in the trash mimicking a basketball jump shot, and walked up to my face.

"Well, let's just say that the price to kill him was outbid by the price to keep him alive."

I seized him by his coat collar and was ready to shatter the mirror above the sink with his head when a customer walked in. The senior citizen wearing a fedora and penny loafers nodded to us on his way to a stall. I let go. Victor smoothed his coat and opened the door.

"I would rethink my allegiance if I were you, Doc."

I did not return his comment as I walked out the door and passed three men sitting in a booth next to the door. They were my former students, Le'Angelo Brooks, Bachari Haids, and Howard Stowe. Room nineteen, row three, seat five; room twelve, row six, seat one, and seat four—desk facing the wall, respectively. Dumbasses. Seeing Le'Angelo again reminded me to find them later and check in on their education, but right now my priority was to kill Osbourne.

What is the price of a strategic alliance with someone you failed to kill, Mr. Goodson? Side-by-side gravesites with your new employer. I sat back down as Della arrived with my usual order, but my appetite had waned. Now I had a taste for blood that Dracula's craving couldn't compare to.

"I—I'm sorry it took so long." Della paused, still holding the lip of my plate, then she exhaled. "That man is the devil."

"The devil," I growled, insulted she gave Osbourne that much credit.

"Excuse me." She looked surprised.

"Della, I suggest you leave—right now."

"Clark, are you okay?"

Distance equals seven meters. *The time is right now. Quit stalling, Watson.*

"Della, I'm telling you to get out now if you know what's good for you."

She looked at me, set my plate down, and walked away, hurried by other orders. My compassion dripped away like a loose-sealed faucet. She stopped behind the counter and whispered to Ruddock, who was cooking. He looked up at me and returned to whisking eggs.

Ruddock is too afraid of insults to speak. I hadn't challenged his education. I would shoot him out of sheer impatience, waiting for him to conjure his voice.

The gooey melted cheese stretched as I speared and lifted Della's eggs with the fork. I was tempted to finish eating my meal, but this was my night. I must complete the mission. I would snap off the bad vine in our community. Death is the successful achievement of circumstance, the eventuality of all choices. It would be my pleasure to shovel the last scoop of dirt on his grave.

Chapter 18

Ava

I heard a bottle roll under the black Caddy parked next to me as three brothers got out of a car, high as a kite and drunk. They didn't even bother to pick up the bottle they threw on the ground—man, they ain't got no respect. Just trash the place and don't care. I hoped whoever owned that car wouldn't puncture a tire reversing out the parking space. *I'll move it before I go in*, I decided. Perform an act of kindness before my sin.

I stared at the gun in my lap and talked to it like it was my pet. I wished it purred like a kitten. I wished I had more spy equipment than just a pen that can record messages. I wasn't sure how to pull this off. All I knew was that I had to be quick about it. Well, quick ain't the word. Osbourne probably had a car parked, waiting for a signal to take out my son. I couldn't lose my baby. I loved my Dazzo.

Scramble

I looked at my gun again for sympathy. It just sat there with the stainless steel shining under the bright yellow-and-white sign that lit up the Waffle Diner. *These things kill more people—Wait, Ava—people kill people with these. I will not take a life. I just need a loan.*

I unlocked the chamber and emptied all the bullets onto the floor mat. The five bullets bounced like jacks on the carpet of the Ford Escort. I shook the pistol. Nothing. Sweat formed on my forehead. Removing a tissue from the compartment between the seats, I uncovered an old photo of me at the community pool. I remembered those days. I smiled, as my heart acted up again. The first day of swimming camp. I checked the time on the analog clock in the middle of the dashboard. I leaned back and sighed, listening to the secondhand tick.

I remembered my mom promising me a whooping when I got home for acting so silly. *Hell yeah, I was crying, Mom. This six-year-old refused to step in that enormous bathtub for anybody. I put my hands behind me in my one-piece bathing suit and shook my head the way my mom taught me to say no to strangers.*

The instructor, a mid-teen redhead, stood next to my mom to assist her in convincing me the water would not swallow me up. I thought otherwise. I had seen the movie Jaws *and knew what lurked below. To hell with that. The redhead hadn't succeeded in stooping to my level to get me into that concrete ocean so my mom intervened. She pointed her finger in my face and reminded me that this was my idea, and I would get my brown behind in the water. Well, I wasn't saying it to my mom, but I damn sure knew I wasn't getting in that water.*

Splash.

It happened so fast. My mom grabbed me and threw me in like a trash bag thrown outside for pickup. I closed my eyes. I did not want Jaws to bite me. The water splashed in my ears, a sound I didn't recognize. It almost sounded like when I tilted my head just right in the shower and the water filled my ear. How could she do that to me? I rose to the top. I started doing what my mom had paid the instructor for me to not do. In a panic, I kicked anything nearby. The water made a hot sensation in my nose. I'm drowning.

"Help!" I fought the water hard, but it fought back something terrible. I cried between my non-rhythmic pattern of kicking and swinging my hands.

Then I remembered.

Relaxing, I opened my eyes not to find myself in the clutches of the shark's mouth, but my instructor smiling at me and my mom with her hands on her hips with a smirk. Hey! An orange vest kept me from sinking. The stinging pain in my nose switched places with euphoria. The instructor kneeled at the edge of the pool.

Scramble

"Kick your legs and move your arms like this."

My instructor did the motions of swimming while I mimicked my newest best friend. I moved toward them, but not fast.

"Good. Now breathe."

After a few kicks, more water splashed in my mouth, and I spit it back into the pool with ease.

"Good girl. Look at you. You're a fast learner." My instructor smiled and clapped.

"That's my baby!" my mom exclaimed.

I made it to the edge by the ladder and stretched for the handles as my mom reached out to me. I grabbed her hand and used her strength to pull myself up.

"I want to do it again. Throw me in again," I yelled.

"See, you did all that crying until you jumped in."

Mom's words snapped me out of my daydream. I cried again as my heart stung in my chest. A robbery? Even if I got the money, I still didn't know who to give it to. Osbourne hadn't left any instructions. I twisted my wrist to check my watch. Only an hour left. *Okay, Ava, get yourself out of this. We can make it through. I will explain later if I have to, but, Ava girl, quit crying and jump.*

I thought of my Dazzo and that red light on his forehead moving around. *Pop.* The door unlocked and I stepped outside my car. Splattered ketchup packets were on the ground with used napkins. That heart of mine thumped, and with each thump, pain shot down my arm.

Lord, help me. Should I really ask the Lord to help me rob the diner? I hid the gun in the pocket of my maroon pullover. As I stepped on the curb and reached for the door handle to the Waffle Diner, I reminded myself to ditch it on the way out. Shit! A lean brother with cornrows bumped me in the shoulder as I walked in. He'd been one of the litterbugs. Crap! I'd forgotten to pick up his bottle. I reached into my pocket to secure my gun. I swear I could see the inside of his head through his large flared nostrils. The handsome man with a nice lean build just looked at me and continued walking.

Brothers ain't got no respect.

I observed Ruddock and Della working as I peeped through the glass windows of the busier-than-usual Waffle Diner. I'd hoped they would both be off so they wouldn't see me do this. Ruddock, the heavyset cook, never said a word the eight years I'd been up there. He just smiled and ate. Della was my favorite waitress. I spent hours there talking and eating my favorite breakfast—Della's Santa Fe Scrambler made with cheese, sausage, green peppers, black beans, onions, and her homemade Santa Fe sauce. I didn't even have to order it. She knew what I wanted when I walked in.

Some days when the bills were hard, Della lied. "*Baby girl, I think you paid already. Now, get out of here before I remember!*"

My mind returned to imagining Dazzo laying on the ground, shot from the gun with that red dot on his forehead. I just needed a small loan. Damn, my heart jolted me with electricity. I was nervous standing at the edge of the pool. My baby, Dazzo! Just like the pool, Ava. Jump in and cry later.

The door creaked open, and my ears filled with the sizzling sounds of fresh sausage mixed with various conversations in the diner. Too many voices, laughter, and drunk-screaming. Hard for me to distinguish one. The smell of pork sausage reached my nose the brief second before I had everyone's attention. Della was the first to see me. She looked tired and sad as she gave a bill to a customer. I watched her eyes grow wide when she noticed what was in my shaking hand. Others joined her in shock, wondering why I had a gun pointed at her and why I was crying.

"Baby, what's wrong? I can get your order ready—"

"Help me—please."

I blacked out. I clenched my chest, fell over, and my gun firing was the last thing I heard. The vibration rattled my right hand. I thought I emptied it, but then there were other gunshots.

Chapter 19

Dr. Watson

I squeezed the handle of my gun in my pocket tighter, being careful not to fire it by accident. I had no more time to calculate.

The next surprise of the evening just walked in. Isaiah Davis's mother entered the restaurant, aiming a gun at Della, and without warning passed out on the floor.

The gun went off when Ava hit the ground, striking Osbourne in the back. Perfect hit. He slumped over, and Vegas stood and pulled his gun as Della and everyone else ducked or ran for cover. I stood facing him and drew my gun as Howard, who was seated between us, pulled out two guns himself. Howard Stowe had graduated from sixth grade eight years ago. Someone sold him a weapon at age nineteen? I couldn't stop thinking of Isaiah Jr. Who is at home with him now? They ruined my shot. I should have fired a round in Osbourne's ass when he first stepped through the door, then left.

Vegas dashed back to Osbourne's side of the table and checked his pulse. Everyone else was running, ducking, or had dropped to the floor, leaving just the three of us standing. I could see a line of sweat sliding down the side of Victor's head. He was nervous.

Isaiah's mom needed attention fast. No one was moving because they were too afraid of being shot. Howard had too much life ahead of him to be involved in this violent activity.

Watson, focus. You have a job to do.

Not now! My mind shouted back. Osbourne would have to wait.

I beat my forehead to hush the voices and their commands that were popping off like fireworks. The plan did not account for Ava getting arrested or killed. I wanted to tutor Isaiah Jr. and be his mentor. Dammit.

"Doc, you're not one for making a commotion like this," Vegas said.

Howard's eyes teetered between the two of us with both of his hands stretched out, guns drawn. His shirt was dripping with sweat in a matter of tense seconds.

"The lady needs help. Put your guns down so we can attend to her," I replied.

"You go first," Vegas pointed to Howard.

"I ain't dropping shit," Howard said, pacing with slight steps.

Della! Where was she? I looked at the cook's station and Della froze, eyes wide like a doe. None of that confidence remained as the longest-tenured server at the Waffle Diner. She was against the fryer with her hands up, her eyes fixed on me and the gun I had pulled. Ruddock was on the floor lying next to her feet, tugging on her dress, trying to pull her out of harm's way.

"The ball is in your court." Victor nodded to me, and now two lines of sweat had formed.

I looked back down at Isaiah's mom. She was breathing, but not moving. Isaiah. I thought of the consequences that would face him for the rest of his life without his mom. I must preserve him at all costs.

Chapter 20

Lee

I told my boys I needed to get some fresh air. I saw Dr. Watson sitting in the booth with that look on his face like he did at the gym the other day. I still don't know why he was so mad about some damn kilograms.

I walked past him into the foyer of the Waffle Diner and collided into this large black woman wearing a hoodie. She fumbled for something in her front pocket when she bumped my shoulder. She didn't even say excuse me. Stupid bitch needs to watch where she's going. I scooted past her and made my way outside.

I reached behind me for my piece in my briefs, secured it, and headed to the back. I saw Osbourne sitting in the booth sipping coffee. I was glad he didn't notice me because I don't fool with him. He never followed up on that offer to work for him, and he doesn't need to. One loan from him taught me enough.

Scramble

On the way back, a garbage truck pulled up to the dumpster where Rogan Stone was running the many cans full of trash from the kitchen to the dumpster. I could shoot him, flip him over in the dumpster, and go back inside to finish my plate of eggs. I dipped below a parked car, pulled my piece out, and sat on the concrete looking up.

Boy, that sounded like gunshots. Was it the Fourth of July? Nah, I'd bet someone just dropped some dishes. I leaned my head back against the car door, looked up past space, and searched for my parents among the stars. I missed them.

That trash truck was getting closer. I heard it again. Maybe it was the brakes, but that whining sound plugged my ears and drowned out everything else. I dropped my gun and put both my hands over my ears to muffle the sound. It was coming from inside. In tears, I leaned over and beat my head against the door. Sitting in the backseat of my parents' 1979 Park Avenue, I looked at my mom next to my dad, and she was shaking her head, apologizing to me. My mom broke my heart all over again with her last look.

That whining sound had me on my hands and knees like a wounded animal trying to crawl away from the fight. Here it comes. A scrambled omelet with Mexican rice, chorizo, beans, con queso, and hot sauce came out of me, onto the ground. I coughed between episodes of vomiting to breathe. *Shit, Della.* I laughed, blaming her again, forgetting about all that Henny I drank earlier. The sound had receded, and I was kneeling in relief. The dump truck was out of sight.

I looked up to my mom and listened for Rogan to empty that last trashcan he dragged out. I counted seven out of eight cans being emptied as I was looking at the stars. When the last one banged on the dumpster, I was right behind him with a .38 stuck at his head.

"Don't look back, or it's over," I told him, smelling the lit cigarette in his mouth.

"I don't have any money, man."

"Fuck the money. Let's go."

"Please don't shoot."

"Shut up! Where's your car?" I asked.

"Over there." He motioned to his right at a blue Chevy Astro van.

"The keys are in my pocket. Here, let me get them—"

I shoved him so hard he almost fell over, but I kept that gun close enough to give his neck a fresh hole if he tried to run.

"Keep 'em. Let's take a ride."

Chapter 21

Ava

"Ava, did you finish your cereal?"

"Yes, Daddy."

It's Saturday morning, and my favorite cartoon is about to come on. I scooped the last of my Froot Loops on my spoon and jammed it in my mouth. Then I tilted the bowl with both hands up to my lips and drank the remaining milk. Yummy!

I love Saturdays. I looked at Mr. Freddy, my teddy bear and bestest friend, and asked if he was ready to go watch TV. I looked at him sternly like my mom, pointing my finger, and then asked if he needed to go to the bathroom. He always wanted to go in the middle of the show. He remained motionless to the human eye, but to my imagination, he spoke a mouthful.

"No, I don't have to go to the bathroom."

"Are you sure, Mr. Freddy, because you always say that and have to go."

"I'm sure, Ava."

"Okay."

I scooted Mr. Freddy's chair back and grabbed him like a baby out of the highchair. I cradled him by the shoulder and skipped into the living room.

"Daddy, cartoons 'bout to come on."

"Okay, I'll be out in a minute." Daddy always put all that whipped cream on his face. It smelled like lemon. Daddy's face got hairy, and he had to shave. He always brushed his teeth, then shaved. My daddy is tall and strong. I like it when he picks me up and throws me above him when we play outside. I always look into his happy eyes.

"Good morning, Ava."

"Morning, Daddy. Mr. Freddy says good morning too."

"Good morning, Mr. Freddy. Shsssh! Let's keep our voices down. Mama's still asleep."

"Right," I whispered. Forgetting he was a real bear, I threw Mr. Freddy on the couch before I jumped up there next to Daddy. Sorry, Mr. Freddy. I sat Mr. Freddy upright and leaned against my daddy's shoulders. He wasn't hurt.

Scramble

I love my daddy. His arms were so big. I ran my finger along his mark on his shoulder.

"Daddy, what's that on your arm?"

"An Omega symbol," he said. "It hurt really bad when I got it branded."

"Daddy, why did you get banded if it hurt so bad?"

He laughed.

"I'm a member of a fraternity, boo-boo," he said kissing my hand.

"What's a faturnity?"

"A club for men and women. If you study hard, you can join one too."

"I am going to be the smartest girl ever."

"I know, Ava." I put my ear to Daddy's belly and heard his stomach rumbling. He rubbed my hair while the music to the Smurfs started to play.

Chapter 22

Dr. Watson

"Bachari! Get her out of here. Did anyone call 9-1-1?" I yelled to the man who was sitting next to Howard. He looked up, shocked that I knew his name, and I nodded toward Isaiah's mom. *I'll challenge his math later*, I thought reflexively. I heard him screaming at Howard, whom he'd called Hardhead.

"Howard, put your gun down—now," I said.

"Hell naw."

"Howard, guns are not the answer. This is." I pointed to my head.

"You got one," he countered.

I looked at Vegas, who grinned.

"You have too much potential for you to die."

Vegas put his hand on Osbourne's neck again, checking for a pulse. His demeanor changed. He must be alive. This must not prosper. He must die.

"Howard, put down the gun. I'm not telling you anymore."

"Doc, you need to make a move, or I'll make one for you," Vegas said as he checked his watch.

"Victor, wait a minute. Let's talk this out."

The third band of sweat ran down his forehead.

"Doc, that's always been your goddamn problem. You can't focus. You have too much on your mind—"

"Damn it, Victor. This isn't the time or place."

"Motherfucker, don't interrupt me."

He shot Howard in the back, right between the shoulder blades, and he fell over in front of us. One gun slid under a booth and the other near my feet. Bachari screamed and dove for Vegas.

"Bachari, no."

I tried to reach in and block Bachari, but I was not fast enough. He stopped when Victor turned and extended his gun right at his head. He looked deep into the dark of his gun barrel.

"You should listen to him," Victor said.

Bachari looked at me. I nodded toward both on the ground. Crying, he walked over to Isaiah's mom and Howard.

"Ruddock, come help Bachari."

Ruddock popped up and assisted Bachari as he hooked his hands under Ava's armpits and dragged her outside. He had to stop a few times to reposition his grip. *Where is the damn ambulance?* I wondered. While Ruddock dragged out a lifeless Howard, a trail of blood made a path out the door following his body. Vegas set his gun on the table to attend to Osbourne.

Chapter 23

Ava

"Daddy, you okay?"

"Yeah, sweetie. Why'd you ask that?"

"You look hot. Are you hot?"

"My tummy's hurting a little bit, but that's it."

"Do you gotta boo-boo, Daddy?"

"Noooooo. Daddy's alright," he laughed.

"Can we get a puzzle today?"

"No, baby. It's not raining, remember? Only when it rains."

The Smurfs came back on! Smurfette was soooo pretty. I liked her long yellow hair. I was about to ask Daddy if he was okay again when I saw his eyes water like he was about to cry. He put his hand on his belly and rubbed it. I do the same thing when my belly hurts. Who's the Smurf with the mirror and the flower in his hat? Oh, oh! Here comes that nasty cat. He's so mean! He's never happy. I hope Papa Smurf turns him into a butterfly. I wish I had a mushroom house. It would be so fun. I laughed aloud when the Smurfs outsmarted that awful cat again.

Chapter 24

Dr. Watson

Education is the most powerful weapon I can use to change the world. I walked closer to finish Osbourne off when Vegas spoke again. Distance equals four meters.

"I will get him out of here before anyone asks questions. I suggest you tend to your friend."

"Are you telling me what to do, Victor?"

"Red, this shit is over. Now I need to get Osbourne to a doctor."

"I can't let you do that." Distance equals three meters.

"What?"

"I can't let you do that. Victor, you're helping preserve a man bent on desecrating the progress of my community. I can't let you do that."

Vegas let go of Osbourne, and he slumped back in the chair. He then stood and lit a cigarette.

"Your community, huh?"

"That's right. His reign ends here, tonight." Vegas puffed with his eyes pointed to the ground.

"Your people, huh?"

"His actions are the source of many problems," I said.

"This solves the problems, right?"

"This is the kick-start we need to move forward," I confirmed.

"We? What 'we'? Red, have you checked a mirror? You are white, Red. A white man. You don't know shit about this community."

"I have done more for this community than Osbourne ever will. He will not prevail," I countered.

"Why, Red? What, because he heads a drug ring? Have you been to Capitol Hill? Motherfucker, everyone is a drug dealer."

"This man poisons my people, Victor, or have you forgotten the struggle?"

"Struggle? What struggle do you have, Red? Tell me. I'm dying to know." Victor picked up his gun. He held it loose in his right hand, shaking it as he spoke.

"I sit in the schools every day, Victor. Drugs are deteriorating the progress of education for this generation of African Americans. My passion is to stop it, and you're in my way."

"Oh, so you stop it, Red, by not allowing the kids to get new computers? Is that your answer? Keep the kids ignorant and in the dark ages?"

"What are you talking about?"

"Osbourne told me how you rejected his offer for those computers."

"He financed those tablets at the expense of someone's addiction. I will not have that on my conscience."

"Red, wake up out of your fantasy world. They founded the United States on corruption. But according to you, it's okay to sell drugs that create addictive behaviors as long as the company is publicly traded, and your fair-skinned gang wears suits? What, drugs are cool if they are packaged in a plastic bottle with a childproof cap and not a plastic bag? What's the difference? Once again, if you were aware of the struggle, as you claim, you would realize those kids who you care so much about need the latest technology despite your clean conscience. You denied those kids an equal footing to suit your comfort level. How does that rest on your conscience, Red?"

"How can you defend a man who doesn't support you or your people, Victor?"

"This man you propose we let die tonight doesn't force anyone to do drugs. People are fucked-up already. They come to him. People that ain't got a future, just like the one I shot. We both know he had a future behind bars, or in an early grave. He made that choice. Quit blaming Osbourne. Who are you to deny his life?"

"I make good on my commitment to the kids if his existence ends tonight."

"Well, motherfucker—" Vegas inhaled and paused. "I'm paid to make sure that doesn't happen. So, what we gon' do, Red?" He flicked his cigarette behind the counter and exhaled his last plume of smoke.

"Don't call me Red."

"You don't focus, Doc."

Victor swiveled his gun to my left and fired. I saw the spark on the edge of the barrel and looked over to see Della pinned against the platinum refrigerator. A bloody red Rorschach test appeared on the right side of her white shirt where the bullet penetrated her small chest. She reached, swinging for air and balance, while I screamed. Victor came back to me and unloaded a bullet in my shoulder. I fell over backward, losing my glasses in the mess of coffee mugs, plates, and food strewn over the floor of the diner. I drew my weapon and shot, hitting Vegas in the leg. He winced and fell over on the table where he had eaten only minutes earlier. Glasses of coffee and plates full of eggs shattered on the ground.

We both laid there breathing heavily in an awful moment of silence. The table rocked as Victor used it to balance, pulling himself up to his knees. He smacked his hand on his bleeding thigh and doubled over in pain.

"Doc," he said, coughing, "the thug didn't mean shit to you, but Della—now what? Something's burning in the kitchen."

I stood, reaching for the twirling stool and grabbed for my shoulder. Blood was pouring out of the wound, and it felt like someone had poured molten steel in my arm.

The trash can Victor flicked his cigarette into had caught fire. The flames were climbing the walls near the storage closet like a frightened cat racing up a tree. I had no time. I had to see if she was okay. I dropped my gun and limped around behind the counter to Della, who was on the floor, still conscious. Shit! I tried to pick her up by her head.

She coughed, and blood filled her mouth. She tried to speak but choked as it bubbled out and down her chin.

"Hang on, Della." I heard Vegas grunting while he struggled, dragging Osbourne. I fought to stand up from behind the counter, cradling Della as I looked at Vegas holding the door slightly ajar. I winced in pain but straightened up to face the man hindering the progress of our people. Both of us were powerful soldiers, protecting what we believed, even to the death.

"Victor, if it doesn't end here, I swear it will end for both of you."

"If you care about your people, then he is your answer. He must succeed."

"Damn you."

The fire surrounded me in the corner near the register and the trash can. The thick smoke created difficulty seeing Victor in the distance. I set Della back down. She was gone.

Death is the successful achievement of circumstance, the eventuality of all choices. It saddened me that her last thought was confusion as to what was happening, and why I had a gun. She would not die in vain. I found my gun on the ground. I steadied my shaking hand and pointed it at Vegas's head. He dropped Osbourne and drew his weapon again.

"He's dead, Clark."

I kept my arm firm, aimed at his forehead. Distance equals five meters.

"That's a lot of money going to waste—a lot of opportunities for my people who died with him," he said, keeping his gun focused on me while he reached in his jacket for another cigarette.

"What you going to do, shoot me? Pull the motherfucking trigger."

Tapping the empty carton, the filter of a square came to surface. He snagged it, dropping the box, and stuck it in his mouth. He reached into his other pocket, revealing a shiny steel square lighter which he flicked with his thumb to ignite a flame.

"I got to do something about this habit. You know, smoking," Victor said after taking a puff.

I remained fixated on where I wanted the bullet to land.

"Pull it," he challenged again.

I remained as I was, calculating the angle to slice his head in half like the story of William Tell—without the happy ending. He took another drag on his cigarette, lowering his arm holding his weapon to blow smoke rings. He laughed.

"Oh, that's right. You can't do a damn thing. You almost pissed yourself shooting me in the leg. That's the problem with the department to which you are so dedicated. All these damn rules set up by our own government-ordered directive."

I grimaced, touching the fresh wound on my shoulder. Sirens getting louder. Victor took another drag and continued unfazed.

"Article five. 'Thou shalt not kill another without the presence of a third for absolute due process,' so that only leaves the tailor. Oh, fucking great! Have fun trying to convince him to kill me. That crazy bastard ain't been the same since that job we had in Mexico City."

The ash on his cigarette grew longer with each word and my patience for listening to him dwindled. I lowered my arm in defeat while the flames shot up around me and Della, her body lying there motionless.

"By the way, I am succeeding Osbourne in his run for office."

"Ignorance is a voluntary misfortune. Don't worry, your fate will be the same as Osbourne's," I said.

Victor Goodson flicked his second cigarette when my gun went off just past his head and shattered the glass behind him. Avoiding the spreading flames, he stepped through the exit created by my bullet, disappearing in the shadows. I limped over to where I fell and found my glasses. After setting them on my nose, I observed the tailor and the butcher through my cracked lenses, standing near the cashier station, surrounded by the growing smoke and flames.

"Your timing sucks, tailor. I could have killed Victor if you'd shown up earlier," I intoned.

"Victor is useless. You, on the other hand, are hard to get a hold of," the tailor replied as his red eyes met mine. Unintimidated, I tried to limp past him when the butcher put his hand in front of me.

"Move your hand or I'll remove it," I warned the laughing butcher.

He's faster than I thought. After seizing my injured arm, he punched me square in the chest. I flew about ten feet on my back. I laid on the ground with my mouth stuck open, unable to catch my breath. My screaming shoulder reminded me of the bullet Victor put in there mere minutes ago.

"Looks like you have a mess on your hands. How do you expect me to clean this up?" the tailor asked as black smoke swirled above him. Rubble tried to fall on the tailor, but he would just move his hand and the debris diverted away from him.

"I don't," I replied, regaining my composure after a few coughs. I made it to my knees and looked up at him as he studied my progress. I used a table for support and hoisted myself up.

"I figured as much. We need to talk. You've been ignoring me, Clark."

"We have no business to discuss."

"Yes, we do. My payment has come due."

The tailor laughed, and his shriek dropped me back to my knees. The cry of the banshee drowned out the approaching sirens of the fire trucks racing here. His screech picked up and cracked the burning walls of the diner. The mark on my face burned through my skin.

"Damn it! Please stop! I don't have time for this now," I pleaded, trying to crawl away. A piece of the ceiling tile fell on me as I tried to escape the shrill of the tailor. I brushed off the piece that landed on my shoulder. The tailor snapped his fingers as I yelped. I couldn't shake off the chunk of the burning support beam that had just knocked me to the ground, pinning my legs underneath.

"Why do you fight me, Clark? Why?" He turned to the butcher who dropped his machete.

"Would you be so kind as to help him out? As much as I'd like to sit here and torture him, we can't. We have a lot to talk about."

Unfazed by the fiery flames, the butcher reached through the fire dancing on the wood and lifted the beam off me, grabbing me by my neck. My feet dangled above the smoldering rubble of the collapsing diner. He laughed and seven pink tentacles reached out his mouth, covering my face as he drew me in for a meal. His tongue comprised of red wine-colored worms that wrapped around my head and neck. The acid from the appendages planted on my face burned my skin, yet I could still see the bloodstains from previous meals on his sharp teeth. His foul mouth full of sharp spears dripped as he pulled me closer. A drop of saliva sizzled on my forehead as I pushed and kicked, trying to resist being drawn in.

"Enough. You will have your meal soon. Set him down," the tailor said.

The butcher grunted as he dropped me to my knees.

"Clark, you see for once we need each other."

The tailor paced as he studied my face. He didn't seem maniacal but did appear to be worried.

"She's free, Clark. Love is free."

"That's not possible. How?" I asked. A sharp pain emanated from my thigh where the beam had fallen on it. Pain raced up my leg as my trench coat caught fire again.

"I don't know how, but she is free. You know she will set Chaos free, and you know what's after Chaos?"

I dropped my head and watched a bead of sweat fall off my chin, then fizzle on the ground under me.

"Do the fucking math, Dr. Watson!"

"The most beautiful song ever heard," I muttered.

"That's right. We are all fucked. With your penchant for avoiding death, you can help me trap Love. In exchange for your services, I might give you what you want the most."

"No, I'm not helping you. We have no working relationship."

"Yes, we do. You owe me!"

The mark on my head began burning again. I grabbed my face with my hands.

"Torture me all you want. I don't care. My answer is no," I said as my face scorched like everything around me.

"You don't get it. This can benefit both of us," he pleaded.

"No. I won't do it," I said.

"Don't you want to die, Enoch?"

I paused as I heard the flames crackle and pop, consuming the surrounding walls. I lowered my hands. Oddly, I felt a beacon of hope from his twisted words in that moment. My doubt ensued; I didn't believe it was possible. A few glass panels shattered as I remained fixed on the tailor.

"Haven't you seen enough? Aren't you tired of living? You fall in love and watch them die. Your friends and loved ones. Babe? You watched Babe suffer from cancer. Why would the government-ordered director do that to you with no explanation? And he was no more? A fucking lie. He didn't take you anywhere. He left you here to rot. It's enough to drive anyone mad," he said.

"How can you kill me?" I asked.

The tailor stepped closer and caressed my chin.

"There are loopholes in everything. Even in the cycle of life and death. I was the gatekeeper. Trust me and I will help you rest in peace."

At that moment, the dormant memory of my wife succumbing to cancer became an active virus in my mind. The other wives I had to bury in my lifetime joined her in torturing me. Companionship was temporary. Death is absolute.

I didn't answer him as he sucked a flame from the wall into his index finger. As the fire raced into his digit, his eyes glowed brighter. Using the fire as ink, he then drew a circle in the air creating a yellow-orange portal hovering between us.

"The police and first responders are in the parking lot. They surround you with no way out. Do you want to spend a few decades outliving your cellmates in jail, taking the heat for all this? Your choice. End your suffering. Help me trap the witch and I will show you how to die."

I looked over at Della's body, burnt to ashes. I winced watching the flames surround her. I promised to avenge her. *Victor will pay with his life. I hope she understands and forgives me for making a deal with the devil.*

The thought of eternal rest, even coming from him, was intriguing. If he is lying, at least I could escape this burning nightmare. My only regret was my concern for Isaiah. I looked at the tailor and nodded in agreement. The butcher picked me up and helped me limp into the flaming gateway as it dissipated into thin air after we stepped through.

Chapter 25

Ava

"Daddy, Daddy, what's wrong?"

"Ava baby, go get your mommy. Daddy's not feeling so good."

I hopped off the sofa to get Mommy. I shook her and shook her until she jumped out of bed.

"Ava, what do you want?"

"It's Daddy. He said he's not feeling good. I think his tummy hurts."

"Honey, are you all right?" Mommy yelled to Daddy from the bed.

Mommy got up and slipped on her house shoes. She grabbed her white housecoat and my hand as we walked down the hall. Mommy looks just like me when I wake up. Her hair was pushed down on one side and she had on no makeup. When we came around the corner from the hallway, we found Daddy slumped over on the couch. Mommy screamed and ran over to Daddy and shook him. She screamed at me to get the phone. She began crying on the phone. I tried to get close, to get Mr. Freddy out of the way, when Mommy told me to go to my room. I started crying and asking what was wrong. She said she didn't know and kept shaking Daddy, but he was still asleep. Then there was a knock at the door. Mommy ran to open the door, and a policeman came in. He rolled Daddy over, but I couldn't see anything because he was standing in my way. I moved over to get a closer look when Mommy screamed at me to go to my room.

Two more strange people came in the house with big bags. I peeked around the corner to see them pushing on Daddy's chest. The lady was holding Mommy, who was very sad. Mommy held a crumpled tissue and she was pushing the lady, trying to get closer to Daddy.

"Please help him," she shouted. When Mommy screams, I get scared.

"Ma'am, we're doing all we can. Please calm down."

The woman in blue pants and a blue shirt spotted me peeking around the corner. She grabbed Mr. Freddy from the couch by Daddy. Those strangers had a box with strings attached to Daddy.

Scramble

"He's not responding!" the man pushing on Daddy's chest earlier said. Daddy shook.

I couldn't hear what they were saying. The woman walked over to me, and I hid behind the wall. She kneeled in front of me.

"Is this yours?" She had Mr. Freddy in her hand. But I want to hold my daddy's hand.

I nodded and I heard them shout "clear" again.

"He's a nice teddy bear. What's his name?" the woman asked.

"Mr. Freddy."

"Oh, and what's your name?"

"Ava."

"That's a nice name."

"Is my daddy okay? We have to watch cartoons today."

"We are trying to wake up your daddy so he can watch cartoons. We may have to take him with us so he can get some help."

Auntie Caroll, from next door, came by to stay with me while Mommy left with the lady who was helping Daddy. Auntie looked so sad.

I played by myself that afternoon because Auntie started crying when the phone rang. She just stayed on the couch and cried. Mommy returned later without Daddy and hugged Auntie. That lady lied. She never brought Daddy home. I never said goodbye.

Chapter 26

Lee

The trees hid like dark ninjas lurking in the approaching fog. Curtains of gray clouds surrounded the paved road, only visible by the yellow stripe being sucked under the Chevy Astro we were riding in. Beyond that, the smoke under the twilight of a crescent moon enveloped my vision, fueling my desire to empty this revolver into Rogan's head at the same place he'd killed my mom and dad.

My broke arm rested in my lap with my gun nestled between my legs. My index finger hugged the trigger, waiting for that moment. A little extra squeeze and it's a closed casket for Mr. Stone, a bloody windshield for this Chevy. I heard the engine moan in the struggle to climb the hill.

Scramble

"I should put a hole in your head now," I said.

"Please, tell me what this is all about?" he asked, only looking at me with his right eye, keeping his neck straight while his hands gripped the steering wheel.

"Shut up and keep driving," I replied, admiring the glimmer of my .38 as we drove under a roadside light.

I felt nauseous again from my dinner of eggs and Henny. *Some things do not belong together, like black men and skis*, I reminded myself, rubbing my belly with my free hand. I watch the dark outline of the trees passing and the occasional headlights from traffic in the opposite lane, using the opportunity to get a closer look at my parents' killer. We were close to the same height, but he outweighed me by forty to fifty pounds. He hadn't shaved his dirty blond head in a while, and he had on a dusty denim cap. The next passing car's headlights revealed Rogan's wide, baffled blue eyes. I'll remind him why we are here. If only my brother could see me now. I'd dedicate his death to my entire family.

I pictured my mom prior to her lying upside down in the ditch, and it broke my heart again. In the windshield's reflection, she peered into the darkness with shoulder-length hair and the extra pounds she carried around her hips after my brother and I were born. Her smile warmed my insides and made me feel terrible all at the same time. I couldn't decide which was doing it to me: Della's eggs or my mom. I couldn't hold it anymore. I remembered when she picked me up after I fell off my bike. How she looked at my scraped knee and my teary face. I told her I'd never ride my bike again. She grabbed my chin and squeezed my cheeks, ordering me to get back on it.

I'd never forget that day because each time I fell off, she made me march right back over and get on it. It was almost as if she enjoyed watching me fall, but I understand now what she did. Life will sure knock a man down, and I had better get back up. Crying over my scrapes wouldn't do a damn thing.

"I'm running low on gas."

"I don't give a shit. Keep driving. Make a left here."

"Where are you taking me? I—I just want to know."

He continued driving. Too bad it's a one-way trip for him. The leaves hit the car like reporters trying to crowd a celebrity limo as we drove along Grace Avenue.

Cherries! Shit!

The flashing lights came up on us in a hurry. Rogan looked out the window while I grabbed for my seatbelt.

"Rogan, if you say a word, it's over. Look where it's at." I dropped the gun between my legs and sat on it. "My aim is good. Don't test it. I can still hit you and this cop, so no funny shit, boss."

"Okay."

He obliged as the cop car sped up, approaching our left side. The warning bumps alerting us that we were too close to the shoulder sent vibrations from the tires to the seat as Rogan veered right, then course-corrected the van. I felt sweat form around my leg and the hand wrapped around the trigger. My cast had all of it hidden, ready to strike at a moment's notice. The officer motioned to the back of our car by frantically pointing behind him several times. Then he turned his lights off and sped forward.

"I forgot about that taillight. I need to get that fixed," Rogan said as he leaned his head back and let out a sigh. I remained silent for a few minutes then looked out my side-view mirror. I chuckled when the same cop car's cherries lit up again a few miles ahead, but this time he did a U-turn and pulled the car over, speeding in the opposite lane.

"I should have called in sick today," Rogan said.

"That wasn't shit," I scoffed. "We get that all the time, except if it was me driving, he would have pulled us over. Try three times in one day."

Rogan said nothing, so I kept talking.

"They'd have me handcuffed, sitting on the ground. He would have searched both of us. I can't believe he only pointed at you. Only thing he would have pointed at me was his gun. It's a wonder black people still smile."

“I guess you want to make a race issue out of this. Most cops are fair. Not all of them are assholes, which most bla—”

The interior of the van lit up as the bullet shattered the driver's side window next to Rogan’s head. The sprinkles hit the ground while the van continued along at fifty miles per hour. Tires screeched as Rogan swerved in his attempt to avoid the attack of glass shards. I yelled over the sound of wind blasting my face.

“I didn’t ask for your fucking opinion. I didn’t ask you to speak. Don’t give me another reason to pull this trigger. I got five more tries to hit your fucking head.”

“It wasn’t fair. That jury was out to get me,” he yelled back.

“What?” I pressed the barrel into the side of his head next to his ear. I was shaking in anger, ready to squeeze my index. The icy wind smacked my face, but I was unaffected.

“Motherfucker, do I look stupid? I put shit together when we turned on Grace. ‘A twenty-four-year-old Happy Canyon man was charged in a double-fatal DUI crash that killed a father and mother at Grace and Soul. The suspect, Rogan Stone, was taken into custody after failing several sobriety checks. The victims were survived by two sons, Jonas and Le’Angelo Brooks.’ I read that article every day I was locked up. That accident ruined my fucking life.”

"Your life. Was ruined," I said. He continued, unnerved by my implied threat.

"Hell, I was at the legal limit. Three beers and a shot. That's all I had. The jury bought into that intoxicated bullshit and didn't look at the facts. It was foggy outside then, just like it is now. That car ran the stop sign and I couldn't stop in time. Not my fault."

"Shut your mouth."

"Fuck you."

Rogan took his left hand off the wheel, reached over, and tagged me in the face. I felt my head bump the passenger side window as he took his other hand off the wheel to lunge for the gun. The car lurched to the right as we approached the intersection of Grace and Soul. I got my finger around the trigger, and Rogan had his hands around mine while we struggled for control. I instinctively braced for the unexpected impact of an oncoming car as the red octagon of the stop sign popped in and out of my peripheral. My hand rattled from the force of a second shot fired.

The steering wheel spun like a ceiling fan on high after we hit the bump. I couldn't feel the engine, but it was screaming at both of us. The bottom of the van was up, then pointed toward the sky and moon. The flips were in between the windshield shattering and the side windows busting out, scattering glass inside the van. McDonald's cups and French fry boxes came flying up front. CDs and tapes did cartwheels, rolling in midair. It hit the ground again. I covered my eyes with my broken arm to avoid contact with the dirt kicked up by the dented frame of the Chevy.

We were sliding down the hill. I watched the gun float like it was underwater, grabbing for it while it hung in front of me. Then it shot toward the back of the car. I heard it ricochet and clang around, bouncing against the steel walls as we flipped again.

Rogan hit the frame and blood streaked across the cracked windshield. I thought he was out. Maybe dead. I lost track of what was going on. My head spun, but my clothes now felt wet. I heard running water like the sound of filling a sink, then my worst fear turned to me. The front of the van pitched forward into a ditch on the side of the road, sinking fast. My seat belt jammed. I kept pulling at it. How was there still no sound?

Help me. I heard my thought, but couldn't move my mouth. I felt the gums on my right side when I tried to bite down and enunciate. My jaw dislocated. I remembered sitting in Osbourne's office and one of his clients had a broken jaw. My thoughts had thousands of intentions, but the crucial one was to get out of there fast.

I looked over at Rogan, still slumped over. Someone had turned the knob on the sink faucet. Water was filling up the van. I moved my mouth back in place after several unsuccessful tries of opening and closing it. Then I heard horses racing over the hill. A thousand horses in a strong gallop around the final lap of the Kentucky Derby. I was still beating and tugging on the seatbelt when the sound became ten thousand horses. It was like a large medieval army. I felt everything shaking. My arm jostled underneath the surrounding cast, shooting pain all over my body. Then ten thousand horses met a million horses, and they all whined. I grabbed for my ears. The sound overtook me. It wasn't horses, but a screaming child. It was the sound of me screaming when I was seven years old.

I was in the backseat of my mom and dad's Park Avenue again, screaming at my dad for making my mom cry. I didn't understand what divorce meant, but my mommy cried after my dad said it, and that was enough to get me fired up. We had just left my grandmama's house, where she'd wanted my brother, Jonas, to spend the night. We were almost home when Mom and Dad began shouting and arguing. I asked them not to fight that night. Well, they ignored my pleas and kept arguing.

"Lee, knock off all that noise before I give you something to cry about," my dad shouted.

"Honey, keep your eyes on the road. It's pretty foggy outside," my mom cautioned.

I kept screaming at him anyway. Jonas looked out the window. I could see the corner of his red eyes as they filled with tears that didn't fall. I saw my mom bury her face in her hands, and that drove the mercury out of the bulb. He turned all the way around and pointed his finger in my face.

"If you don't shut up crying, I'm coming back there and—"

"Jonathan, look out," my mom screamed.

"Oh, shit!"

Those were the last words I heard from my dad. The impact of the blow from Rogan Stone's Chevy Nomad jolted my dad out of his seat. Then we were rolling over. My dad hit the steering wheel and driver side window. My screams drowned out everything. Mom looked at me, shaking her head with eyes full of tears. The front of the car began sinking, and my mom and dad were soon swallowed in the chocolate. I was getting closer to the water in my seat when a voice called, so familiar to me.

"Hey, honey, give me your hand."

Della, my favorite waitress at the Waffle Diner. I looked to my right, and a woman covered in mud up to her uniform apron reached out to rescue me. She was young and wrinkle-free. That same bright fire-engine-red hair. Celery green eyes. I asked her to help my parents. Della shook her head and stepped in closer to pull me out. I reached for her and felt guilty—guilty I was too young to save my parents from their fate.

"Let me get you out first, Lee."

I stretched toward her. She pulled a knife out to cut me free, and time put me back in the van.

A switchblade on the roof of the interior slid towards me. I reached for it and sliced through the seat belt. I was soaked, my tank top now a dark brown. I used my cast to bust out the remains of the windshield. I was getting stuck. The mud rose to my chest. Rogan's head was submerged in the bog he fought to escape. The van was sinking too fast for me to grab him. Two legs approached the other side and stooped down.

"You okay in there?"

"Jonas?"

"Lee?"

"Get me out of here!" He stepped closer and squatted down to pull me out through the front of the wreck before it sunk past the hole in the windshield.

I rested my hands on my knees, sucking in deep breaths.

"You okay?" he asked.

"I'm okay."

"I called the police. What about your friend in there?"

"Not my friend, but try to lift the van so I can reach for him. To get him out."

"Who is it?"

"Don't ask. Help me."

"Okay," he said, pushing against the side of the Astro while I laid down to go after Rogan. A spike of glass cut into my belly as I strained towards him. The screaming sounds died. Rogan's hand unclenched, grasping for life. I couldn't grip enough of his hand to pull him. I watched the water swallow his fingers. I scooted back outside.

"Let's try again. C'mon, Jonas!"

Exhausted, with mud up to our knees, we pushed. The fog rolled in, thick as a curtain. Frogs and crickets were screaming in the night. I had to look twice because I thought a woman was on the top of the overturned van. I looked back at her, but no one was there.

I didn't have enough strength with one broken arm to move anything. We tried again, giving it everything we had, but the van only moved an inch after all that effort.

We heard a yell and turned to see a highway patrol officer sprinting down the hill, leaving his car with flashing blue and red lights behind. His wide-brimmed hat flew off while his blue uniform became soaked with mud as he kicked up the shit water in his mad dash to us.

"Someone in there?"

"Yes, sir. It suddenly ran off the road," my brother said, nodding at me.

"Let's switch. I'll try to get him," the trooper replied.

I had my back to the van holding it up, and Jonas was pushing with his hands in the mud, struggling to keep his balance. I could feel my feet sinking deeper into the quagmire.

Glancing down at my tank top, I noticed new red and pink splotches from the bleeding cut. *Push harder.* The van moved. The front edge lifted, creating a small space. Water droplets sounded like a leaking gutter on a rainy day as the raised front end dripped on the wet marsh. The cop stooped lower in the mud and with a stretch to the end of his fingertips, fished Rogan's muddy hand from the seat, dragging him through the jagged windshield.

Now on the dry side of the hill, the cop started pushing on his chest. Fifty chest compressions and four breaths later, Rogan gasped, spitting up mud. The cop turned him on his side so he could vomit, then reassured us that help was on the way. Saving his life didn't feel right. I felt conflicted at this, but then I thought of Grandmama and what she would want us to do. Jonas put his arm around me. Alive.

Minutes later, Jonas ran up the hill to the row of flashing lights, greeting the first responders who'd arrived. I stayed down in the ditch, drowning my memories for the last time. I asked the cop if he was ok. He affirmed, then continued to provide rescue care for Rogan as the EMTs hurried down the slope.

I didn't understand what the hell Jonas was doing here, and was positive he wondered the same thing about me. Holding my stomach in pain, I climbed up to where he stood. I heard the signature beeps of a tow truck backing up off the highway onto the shoulder in front of the row of police cars. Jonas was explaining to the officer what happened.

"Sir, I talked to you before. I come out here often to think and reflect on my parents. I brought my brother this time. We were both sitting—"

"I know you. That's right. What did you see?" the cop asked.

"The van came by and ran off the hill. It happened so fast. Couldn't tell how fast he was driving."

"Okay, here is my card."

He noticed me holding my bleeding belly.

"Tough night. That fog has caused several wrecks in this area. You two did an excellent job down there. The ambulance will take him in. Get that cut looked at. We can firm up the events later."

I looked back to the ditch, relieved to be saved, when my eyes caught that woman standing on top of the car again. I could make out her inky hair and tattered dress. I blinked, and fog concealed the overturned van. Damn, this Hennessy was screwing with my head. I looked at my brother.

"Can you take me to the hospital?"

"I'm right here with you, bro."

Chapter 27

Lee

"Gangsta . . . Gangsta Lee, the town hero?"

"Rogan?"

"Who's Rogan?"

"Where am I?"

"Man, gangstas sleep all the time. What's up, Lee? How are you feeling?"

I focused my blurred vision, confirming that the rotten smell belonged to Neru's breath. The itch I could never seem to scratch held a cup of coffee and his breath held my fresh air hostage. He sat with a big grin in a chair at the foot of the couch I was lying on. *I'm at home? How?* I tried sitting up and fell back down on the cushion. Ouch. My stomach hurt from the stitches.

"Who drove me back to the hospital?"

"Drove back?"

"I left last night."

"You got the 'left' part right. Don't you remember you and your brother found that guy in the ditch yesterday? You drink too much, man. Gangstas and alcohol. A terrible combination."

The events that happened unfolded in my mind like wings on a bird. Jonas found me. He covered my ass, explaining what happened to that officer.

Simi walked in with Juni holding Jonas's hand. Juni smiled at me.

"Hi!" She ran up to the foot of my couch and tried to jump on it to play. I thought of tossing her out the window, which made me smile.

"Juni, stop. He's hurt." She stayed near the edge and pulled out her coloring book on the table.

Jonas walked in and handed me the newspaper.

"Hey, Jonas, I'm sorry about yesterday—"

"Did you get a look at the paper? The Waffle Diner burned down the same night—" He glanced over at Neru, "—that we found that guy."

"What? What happened?" I sat up. Ouch. I winced again, clutching my stomach packed with gauze and surgical wrap.

“No one has the same story. A robbery, assassination. It’s a rumor mill on the street. They found a few bodies.”

“Della. Is she okay?” I asked.

“Don’t know. They have to ID the other bodies.”

Jonas turned away from me. *No, not Della.* I grabbed the front page of the paper and read. *Damn, Hardhead too?* Several shots were fired in an attempted robbery that killed Osbourne. The one man in St. Louis no one fucks with, now dead. The man I was so afraid of, I’d robbed a grocery store to pay him back his loan.

Jo turned away and looked out the window of the living room. I tried to piece this together. Simi and Neru moved their lips, but I tuned out their sounds and I remembered Rogan going down with the van. I did my best to save him. The memories of what happened to my mom and dad had risen to the surface when we drove over the hill. I refused to let anyone else die the way my parents did.

I breathed out a deep sigh and recalled Della grabbing me from the sinking car so many years ago. She’d stayed with me until Grandmama arrived. I wished I could reach for her now and get her out of that burning building. With so many strange people at the accident scene years ago, she was the only one who’d comforted us. Jonas and I owed so much to her. From her brilliant advice to losing our dinner bill when she knew we didn’t have the money. I wiped my tears on my arm.

"That guy in the van didn't make it, either. Swelling on the brain."

I said nothing.

"Was that who I think it was, Lee?"

We sat in silence while Neru helped Juni color. A few minutes later, he walked over and took my hand that wasn't in a cast.

"Lee, they charged that woman who hit you with reckless driving." Neru tugged on his dreadlocks. "I—I—I wanted to—ummmm— well, my daughter is sitting here with us, thanks to you."

Neru paused and teared up again while looking away. Simi handed Neru a tissue.

"Let me finish. Lee. After you saved her, I think that hit from the car might have triggered trauma from your past. You probably have PTSD. I work with counselors who can help you work through that. Let me set up a few appointments this week. I know it can be scary to talk to a therapist, but I can—we can go with you."

"Okay, I want help."

Neru squeezed my hand. I'd had nightmares for a long time. I hoped they could help me, but right now my insides were turning at the thought of someone else I cared about being gone. But not my brother. He's here. I felt that sharp pain when I tried to sit up. He put his hand on my shoulder.

"Jonas?"

"What's up?"

"Why were you there?"

"I'm always there. After we fought at the hospital, I stopped by there to meditate. I sit, and I think about things. Ask Mom and Dad what they would do in certain situations. Pray. Talk to Grandmama."

I was about to ask him about the car when he cut me off.

"That night of mom and dad's accident, I didn't know what to do. I made it out the car and all I could think of was to get help. I left you in there because I didn't think the car would sink. It must have started after I left. I ran up that hill and down the road to wave someone down. I was screaming and crying when Della pulled up. She put me in her car and told me to stay while she would try to help."

"Hey Lee, Jonas, we can leave, man." Neru and Simi started gathering their things when Jonas stopped them.

"No, Neru, you are family too."

One tear ran down his face.

"I'm sorry, man. Della came back up with you in her arms, crying when she put you down. She just kept saying she was sorry to us. She sat and waited for the police and Grandmama to come.

So much mud was on her dress and then your sobs. I felt helpless. Here I am, twelve years old. And I've punished myself every day since then for not saving our parents. Still to this day, I think back to what I could have done that night." Jonas clasped his hands and looked at me. The one tear became two tears racing down his face.

"You did the right thing, bro. I didn't know. I understand now."

Neru walked over and put his arms around my brother. My face was wet. A little.

"So, that's what I do," Jonas said. "I go down there and try to find peace and acceptance when things in life go awry. I wanted to kill Rogan too when he was released. I had to sit first. My place to go to remind me I might have lost my parents and Grandmama, but I still have family. It scared the daylights out of me when that van tumbled down the ditch. Come to find out you were in it. Well, I am glad I was there because this time around I didn't lose anyone."

"Amen," Simi said.

"Mind if I tag along to see that counselor?" Jonas asked holding my shoulder.

"Let's do it. We are family, Jonas," Neru said. "You, and your brother."

"Can Uncle Darvin come over when he's feeling better?" Juni asked, coloring her new picture of me with a thick ass green crayon. Neru winked at me, and I had to grab my stomach laughing in pain.

"Darvin, huh? Your dad put you up to that shit, didn't he?"

Chapter 28

Ava

"My principal told me to give this to you," Dazzo said, sitting at the edge of my bed. I had a tube going down my nose and I heard the beep of a heart-monitoring machine. My baby was still alive. Osbourne didn't kill him. *What happened? Why am I here?* It was blurry and I couldn't piece it together.

Dazzo handed me an unmarked envelope. I winced from pain as I opened it. A check fell out along with a letter. So much money. More than I'd ever seen in a check.

Dear Ms. Minnow,

We must continue to invest in our children. With the challenges that lie ahead of them, we cannot afford to let them lack for any of their needs, which may prevent them from achieving a quality education. We must support parents. It is vital to the success of our people. The new struggle is not with pickets and songs on Washington. We must succeed with a powerful family and insert ourselves in positions to reach down and pull each other up. I feel moved to invest in Isaiah, as I expect to see a great many things from him in the future. God extends rarity to a single grain of sand; custodians of universes alike. Isaiah's life depends on how well he succeeds academically. Please put some of this away to use for his higher educational pursuits. I hope this investment will assist you. I overheard you mention to "Dazzo" that you are financially stretched right now. We can win this war, one child at a time.

Dr. Clark Watson

Well, thank you, Lord! I set the letter down and looked at Dazzo, snuggled in the crook of my mother's left arm. I held the check up and counted the zeroes. Thank you, Jesus! I'd put enough away, so by the time he graduated from high school, he'd at least have enough to begin college. The house. I have enough for the down payment on my dream home.

Later that afternoon, the doctor told me I had experienced a mild heart attack. He referred me to a nutritionist and prescribed medication. The doctor said I was lucky I'd received medical attention in time. My neighbor Bachari was at the diner right when I'd walked in and passed out. He dragged me out and drove me to the hospital. I thought about the check from Dr. Watson. What do you give someone for saving your life?

Isaiah Sr. was recovering, I learned. He told me that Osbourne died at the diner that same night. They found his body in the piles of bricks, tables, and burnt plaster after the Waffle Diner burned to the ground.

Isaiah broke the news that Della died in there, too. My sadness overwhelmed me and I waited for the tears to cease. I will miss Della. She was such a warm person. I remembered going to visit her at the diner often, even on days when money was tight. On those days, she always seemed to misplace our bill for dinner. I wished I could pay her back. Maybe I'd make her a garden of flowers when they clear away the debris. I hoped she wasn't an innocent bystander of whoever killed Osbourne. I would like to thank the person who stood up to him.

Hunter stopped by as soon as I thought to call him. He thanked me over and over for my spy job in the bathroom at work. His boss told him I'd risked my job to expose the truth. I almost had another heart attack when he said he wasn't planning on returning to work, despite the offer of his job back. He wanted to focus on his dream of being a full-time personal trainer. I asked if I could be his first client. Get my heart in shape so we can stay out of hospitals.

In the hospital, I learned heart disease ran in my family. My daddy died from it. It's waiting for me too if I don't change my ways, but I'm determined to live to see Dazzo graduate.

I reached in my purse and pulled out my journal. I found my bent page with the picture of my dream home. Pasadena Hills Fine Homes & Townhouses. I imagined my eggshell-white two-bedroom starter home, and a beautiful sunset. The photo wrinkled in certain pages, but it looked so real to me now. So possible.

I pulled Dazzo in for a kiss on the forehead and laughed as he struggled to get away. Then I folded the principal's check and placed it inside my journal, next to my future home. I thanked the Almighty before drifting off to sleep with my journal tucked in my folded arms.

"Good morning, Daddy."

"Hey Ava, boo boo!"

"Daddy, it's raining outside."

"C'mon in the front room. Your favorite cartoons are on."

I raced in the living room at top speed and shot into my daddy's lap.

"I have a surprise for you."

He pulled a puzzle from behind his back. Oh boy! The cover was a little girl with an umbrella in a wheat field. You couldn't see her face because her back was turned. I beamed while he opened the box, scattering all the pieces on the table. My mom was in her favorite chair reading. She would often look up and smile at us. I could hear rain falling outside while I sat with Mr. Freddy and my daddy on a Saturday afternoon putting together our puzzle.

Chapter 29

Isaiah Davis, Jr.

"Before I tell you about what I'm here to tell you, I want to share a little story. When I was about your age, my mama had a heart attack in the middle of a diner. They got her to the hospital, and you know what, she was up and fine that next morning. I rode home later that day with my dad, happy that she was okay, not realizing that was the last time she would kiss me. She just took a nap and never woke up. Nothing was ever really the same after she left the earth. My biggest regret is that I couldn't help her get that dream house she always talked about and she didn't get to see me walk across the stage to get my degree.

"That's why it was important to me that I get an education and make something of myself. It's what she would have wanted. I enrolled in Wilberforce University, even got a partial scholarship, and six hard years later, I graduated. I didn't have top honors, but I did the darn thing, and I'm proud of it. Now I'm an engineer for the water company, and I'm responsible for service installation, design, and maintenance for both business and residential customers. You know that bath your mama makes you take before bed? That's because of me," I smiled, as the children tittered in front of me. "Oh, one other thing people find interesting about me… You know Juni Khudjan? From Fox3 News? She's my girlfriend. Well, that's me in a nutshell. Does anyone have any questions?"

A kid wearing a Raptors jersey raised his hand.

"Man, I can't stand school. It's too hard. I don't feel like studying. I'd rather play basketball."

The class laughed.

"Class, hush right now. Mr. Davis is speaking," my former teacher, Miss Colwell, said with a tone that brought back memories of receiving her discipline.

"He actually made a great comment. It's the truth. School is hard. Life is hard, but knowing that life is difficult helps make it easier. Make sense? I watched my mama struggle to make ends meet. We didn't have a lot, but she sacrificed what she wanted to put a roof over my head, and food to eat. There were so many other people cheering for me to succeed. After she died, I was determined to finish." I looked out into their young eyes and used a firm voice.

"You just can't go out there and be a Vince Carter. He had to work to get into the Hall of Fame. Practice, practice, and then more practice. He was gifted, but a gift without dedication is a wasted present. Talent plus investment equals strength. It's the same thing with school. The biggest reward comes with the hardest work because not everyone is dedicated enough to finish the task." I focused now on Raptors Jersey, "Whatever you decide to do, know that it takes sacrifice, dedication, and effort. Go for your dreams, little man. Your life depends on it. Shoot for the stars, and you'll at least hit the moon."

The bell rang, ending Career Day at my old school. I received several high-fives from the kids as they walked out. Miss Colwell reached for the top of the blackboard with her eraser. She still looked the same, except for the new wrinkles on her face. Time has aged both of us. Man, it seems to go by so fast these days.

"Well, Isaiah, you sure have come a long way. Your mom was such an inspiration to me."

"She did what she had to do. I'm always grateful. Now I'm trying to give back to as many kids as I can."

"It was a pleasure having you as one of my students. You never gave me trouble since—"

She turned away, embarrassed, but I didn't see a reason for her to be. I laughed, thinking back to the day I called her a bitch when she gave us extra homework. I didn't know it was such a bad word; I'd heard my mom use it on the phone with her friend like there was no tomorrow. And I heard my pops calling Mama a bitch when he was drinking with his boys playing poker. I thought it was cool. I quickly learned otherwise, thinking of the many "lessons" on my behind.

"I apologize again for disrespecting you," I offered.

"You were young. And, I'm a teacher. I've been called worse. Well, do you have any big plans for yourself?"

"I want to travel, then I'm right back into my studies. I have to get my master's, but I'm not sure if I want to tackle math or engineering. For some reason, I'm leaning towards math."

"It will come to you. I've learned over the years that getting an education usually takes a lifetime. Don't always assume that a piece of paper is the only means of saying that you have an education. The earth itself teaches a lot of lessons. Thank you so much for coming to my career day."

"Well, I'll plan to see you next year," I said.

As I was leaving, I made sure to greet the secretary, Ms. Hall. She still looked smoking hot after all these years. Time hadn't aged her like Miss Colwell.

My phone rang at the same time I voice-commanded my vehicle to start. I heard the engine purring under the hood as I walked out the doors of Happy Canyon Elementary. I laughed thinking of my mama's primitive phone. A keypad? I hadn't seen keypads or touchscreens in years. I could imagine the number of accidents caused by people trying to dial on the highway. This microphone could pick up my voice from twenty feet away. My phone spoke to me and I spoke to my phone.

"Sup, homie?"

"Romie, what's shaking, baby?" I responded.

Rome—Roman Calle—my best friend from as far back as I could remember. We grew up together; his mom and my mom were best friends and we'd been tight since day one.

"Man, chillin' like a villain, man."

"Man, you're talking like it's the nineties again."

"Dude, I got the new hologram theater."

Hologram home theaters had been created by Spins Inc. The founders were local heroes, having grown up here in North St. Louis. Bachari Haids and Le'Angelo Brooks had started out like most men in the hood; rough circumstances, trying to overcome and make it. Now they were the leaders in factory after-market accessories for cars and home theaters. They even decorated celebrity interiors. What really put Spins Inc. on the map was a technology breakthrough made by Bachari's fiancée, Arina Jacobs. She discovered how to project an image in three dimensions anywhere. Word on the street was that next year they are going to translate the technology into mobile devices.

Arina sold her patent to Samsung for fifty million dollars plus royalties, and is credited with the death of the flat-screen television.

"Man, I bet that looks crazy."

Rome crowed, "Bro, you are *in* the movie! No headsets or nothing. It's like you are in the scene. You got to check this out."

"You ain't gotta tell me twice," I said putting my briefcase in the trunk.

"Bro, did Juni find out what's up with that weather lady? Hook ya folk up, Daz."

"Which one? Maria?"

"Don't even play like that. I'm talking about Dion Wheels."

"Man, quit talking. You ain't ready to be her sugar daddy."

"With her, I would settle in a heartbeat."

"I'll see if I can set up a happy hour and put you two in the same room. Anyway, I'll be by to check out Rambo. I'm headed to my—"

As I slammed my trunk door, it felt like someone pushed a pipe through my back. I heard my phone hit the ground. I tried to turn, but I was met with resistance. I raised my hands and tried to peep over my shoulder.

"Don't make a fucking move."

"My wallet's in my pocket."

"I don't want your wallet."

"Please, sir, what do you want?"

"I'm asking the fucking questions around here. Do you fucking understand me?"

Shit! Of all the days and in all the places to be robbed—my elementary school on career day. The man's rusty voice sounded familiar.

"Answer them right and you will live. Understand?"

When I didn't respond, he jabbed the gun into my back.

"Understand?"

"Yes, sir."

"Question one." He coughed a few times then cleared his throat. "You get your wallet out because you are being robbed and you accidentally drop it. How fast is it accelerating towards the ground?"

"What?"

The gun dug deeper into my back. He started coughing again.

"I have a bullet for each kidney… now answer me."

"It would be 32.2 feet per second per second."

"Do you think you're a comedian? I hate imperial units. My patience is growing thin."

"It's 10 meters per second squared," I answered.

"Question two: You have fifty, one-dollar bills, making the total mass 250 grams. What is the force opposing the wallet as it is falling to the ground?"

"Zero. The wallet is in free fall. There are no opposing forces, making the simplifying assumption it's falling in a vacuum. Do you want me to calculate the resistance due to the drag force of the air?"

He grunted, "No, that's good. Good. Now, what is the gravitational force on the dropped wallet as it's falling towards the ground?"

I lowered my hands slightly, and he poked me again.

"Isaiah Davis, answer the goddamn question," he demanded.

"It's two and a half newtons."

"Incorrect answer, Isaiah. You disappoint me."

While the muzzle was still in my back, he cocked the gun.

"Did you convert the grams to kilograms, Dr. Watson?"

He remained silent for a minute, then he continued. "Good observation. Tell me the gravitational potential energy of the wallet if it falls out your back pocket to the ground?"

"But Dr.—"

He rammed the muzzle into my back again.

"I have no time for your shit. Answer the god-damn question."

"Assuming my pocket is one meter above the ground, 2.5 joules."

I felt the gun ease off my spine.

Now the last question: How much—"

"The kinetic energy is initially zero and increases with the increase in velocity of the wallet. All the gravitational potential energy at the beginning of the fall will be converted into kinetic energy, thereby making the final kinetic energy of the wallet, right before it hits the ground, *also* 2.5 joules. Once it hits the ground, the wallet's velocity decreases to zero, and because I like my money, I would pick it up as soon as I could."

He stood behind me in silence. I had been preparing for this day since our lunch encounter all those years ago. My mom wasn't the only motivating force in my life. Dr. Watson made it a matter of life or death that I knew my shit, and now that I'd gotten older, I understood that education is a matter of survival. That's something I didn't play with.

I'd read his letter with the check he gave my mom before she died, and I knew then there were too many people depending on me to succeed. I studied my ass off every night. Thanks to him and my scholarships, I received a quality education at a top school. A dream for many. I prepared for this day, not expecting to die, but waiting to say thank you for what he did. As I got older, the thought always nagged at me, though. What could he possibly see in me all those years ago? God only knew the path I would have taken if he had not made studying a priority.

"I made a wise investment in you after all. I'm very proud."

"Thank you, Dr.—"

I turned to thank him, but he was gone.

Scramble

www.ingramcontent.com/pod-product-compliance
Lightning Source LLC
Chambersburg PA
CBHW060820310726
48980CB00002B/348
9780578702131